It's A Dirty Job...

Writing Porn For Fun And Profit

ISBN 1-929072-23-6

Manufactured in the United States of America.

It's A Dirty Job...

Writing Porn For Fun And Profit

Katy Terrega

Booklocker.com

It's A Dirty Job...

Writing Porn For Fun And Profit

Preface..   1
Introduction   3

I   SOME BASICS
      Can You Write Porn.   5
      Following Your Conscience.   15
      Tools of the Trade:.   19
      Taking Care of Business   23
      Choosing Your Pseudonym.   29

II   BEFORE YOU BEGIN
      Doing Your Homework.   35
      The Magazine Formats: Letters, Stories, Non-Fiction   41
      Some Additional Markets.   45
      Manuscript and Query Basics.   49
      Staying Focused.   57

III   THE ART OF WRITING PORN
      Who, me? Write?.   61
      The Basic How-To.   65
      But It's All Been Done Before   75
      Characterization   77
      Plotting.   81
      Ideas.   85
      The Real Secret Behind Good Ideas.   89

IV   STORY SPECIFICS
      Letter Basics.   97
      Anatomy of a Three Thousand Word Story.   101
      The Non-Fiction Article.   113

V   Working With Editors.   121

VI   Never, Ever Give Up.   127

VII   Now Go For It!.   133

VIII Paying Porn Markets.   135

IX   Non-Paying Markets.   155

X   Writer's Guidelines   157

Preface

The debate rages on. Is it porn or is it erotica? Is it hardcore or is it softcore? Is literature or is it...well...smut? Does it really matter?

It all boils down to a basic fact of life: Sex is sex; as old as life and just as compelling. We seem to be insatiable in our need to dissect it, to understand it, to revel in it. We like to read about it, think about it, and, as often as possible, *do* it. Whatever form it takes, whatever words we choose, sex is hot. And sex sells.

Whether we're talking literary erotica or hard-core pornography, it can be written about and it can be sold. So, for the purposes of learning how to write and sell written sex, we'll just cut to the chase and call it porn. You can decide for yourself whether you want to be a peddler of porn or a literary eroticist. Whatever you decide to call it, I can almost guarantee that you'll have fun writing about it and your audience will have fun reading about it!

Introduction

You'd never know just by looking at me. Keeping my somewhat questionable career choice to myself, I manage to present myself as a relatively typical work-at-home mom. Yes, the ancient art of writing does have a long and (mostly) respected history, but the kind of writing that I do tends to be rather *dis*respected in this polite society. There are many who would even consider it blasphemous in the extreme to include what I do in the same realm as the sacred category of ...(hush) ... *Writing.*

But that's okay. I am what I am. Porn Writer (as well as Mom) is just one of the many hats that I choose to wear, although I am rather careful about who I tell. Only a select few know what I *really* do after I kiss my kids goodbye at the classroom door. And even they don't know (and probably don't *want* to know) the details – that I trot on home each morning to a computer with file names like 'Lesbian Tendencies' and 'How to Introduce Your Lover to the Joys of Kinkier Sex.'

Some might question how one can be a mom and a feminist *and* a literate woman and still write mainstream porn. The truth is, I actually enjoy the challenge of creating sensitive, caring characters within this generally exploitative genre. I look at it as almost a community service. Yes, it may be a dirty job but who *else* is going to spread the word? Sometimes I even go so far as to consider it my calling.

And as callings go, it's really not all that farfetched. Write what you know, say all the experts. Well, gosh, I know how to have sex, I know how to fantasize and I know how to write. Voila! Career choice option number one, please! And s a career choice, you sure can't beat this one for pure fun.

Think about it. How hard is it to imagine your wildest fantasy, embellish it a little or a lot, write it down and get paid for it? How hard is it to peruse lingerie sites on your home computer in the middle of the afternoon? And how hard is it, really, to try out that taboo little sex act, the one you've always been curious about, all in the name of research?

Fact is, writing porn is fun. It's also one of the easier markets to crack and make money at while you're still honing your skills. All you need to do is check your inhibitions at the door and we'll show you how to do the rest.

I
Some Basics

Can You Write Porn?

Despite the common assumption that porn is so simplistic that anyone can write it, not everyone is suited to this particular genre.

Porn is not for those uncomfortable with its graphic nature and it's most certainly not for the squeamish or the faint of heart. A genre totally unto itself, porn demands an uncommonly open mind and a willingness to experiment. While erotica can and often does have undertones of romance and love - common themes for a lot of writers - porn just as often does not. Porn writers are, depending on your source, either scraping the bottom of their most basest perversions or accessing the highest levels of their imaginations. Either way, those with closed minds need not apply.

But even for those with admittedly open minds, there are still a few prerequisites for the successful writing of porn. Ask yourself these questions: Do you like to read it? Can you handle the prejudices and preconceptions inherent in the genre? Are you enough of a free thinker to be able to create stories out of fantasies that you may have previously deemed too shocking? Answer in the affirmative to any of the above and you may well have what it takes to tackle this exciting but very specific market.

Just like other narrowly defined markets (think romance or science fiction), your chances of being able to write porn are much better if it's something that you already enjoy reading. For example, while researching the craft of romance writing I found that the prevailing advice was to read not just a few current and past romances but dozens or more. Along with the caveat that if just the *thought* of undertaking such a chore was daunting, then perhaps romance writing was not the job for you. At first I have to admit that I was rather taken aback by such advice, mainly because the thought of reading dozens of romances didn't particularly appeal to me. Aw, come on, couldn't I read just a few and pick up the basics?

Well, sure, but only if I was willing to settle for being a poor to mediocre romance writer. Fact is, if you want to be better than that, if you want to actually be *good* at what you do (or have any fun at it), you had better enjoy it. I happen to love reading porn. It also happens to be extremely easy for me to write. Mere coincidence? I think not. It might be stating the obvious to say that if you've rarely looked at or read porn, it's probably not going to work for you.

Of course, simply liking it may not be enough. Porn writers also have to sometimes deal with the more controversial aspects to the writing/reading of porn. Like, what will the neighbors/family/boss think? There are plenty of societal as well as moral implications peculiar to this genre. For some people the distinctions are clear, porn is either okay or it's not (and I pretty much have to figure that if you're reading this book you fall into the former category). For the rest of society there are plenty of murky areas.

Yes, there are those people who are relatively porn-neutral; those who don't tend to buy the stuff but acknowledge its place as a benign entity in others' lives. My husband falls into this category. Until I came along and, um, forced him to read my stories, he could count on one hand the number of times he'd perused smut magazines. It was not that he disliked them or thought them to be bad. He simply wasn't interested.

But he happens to be the exception. The vast majority of people seem to fall into two extreme categories: There's the porn-friendly crowd, which ranges from the adamant, fist-shaking, first-amendment-rights-declaring pornographer to the sleaze-ball down the street to the parent of three who rather guiltily stows his or her collection in the top drawer of the dresser. These kinds of people may be surprised when they learn what you do, or intrigued or even downright interested, but they likely won't judge you too harshly.

Then of course there are the porn-haters, although they, too, can range from the religious picketer of porn shops to the self-righteous do-gooder down the street to the disapproving businessman who's never read a sentence of the stuff but still wouldn't be caught dead peering at a Playboy. I tend to avoid these kinds of folk in general but you never know. Is the father of my child's playmate a free thinker or a card carrying anti-pornographer? More for the sake of my kids than anything else, I'm not about to share my profession with him just to try and find out, thank you very much.

Unfortunately for the porn writer, there are many people out there who think that pornography is evil, or at least very, very bad. These often harsh opinions and attitudes are part of what you, if you choose to take porn on, are going to have to deal with. There are those who will think less of, or at least differently about *you*, knowing that you participate in such a venture. It can be frustrating having a career that you can't talk about to your neighbors, your friends or your children. Can you live with the secrecy, the occasional deception? Can you live with the fact that you will be judged, sometimes positively, oftentimes harshly?

And speaking of harsh, there are plenty of *writers* out there who take a pretty dim view of pornography. Many of them don't accept my own personal assessment that porn is a legitimate form of writing. I've found, when dealing with self-proclaimed *real* writers, that I'm sometimes treated as though I participated in other, shall we say, less legal sexual professions.

I've often felt like an errant and out of favor stepchild when communicating with published as well as unpublished mainstream writers. There've been several who have suddenly and without explanation disappeared from my life after they've discovered what form my writing takes. And I've had more than a little trouble getting my book reviewed by some of the more literary venues.

Even when I do finally make it into their realm, the reception has often been less than welcoming. In one negative review, the reviewer didn't actually find fault with the quality of the book or the writing. She did however talk dismissively of one who would "whore (their) writing talent to the porn industry." It was quite clear how entirely unacceptable this genre was to her and her ilk.

In the end, writing porn is probably not going to win you any awards or kudos unless you tackle literary erotica. There, if you're really good, you may find a place among the vaulted. But down here in the trenches it's just us lowly porn writers.

So much for what other people think. There are also your own attitudes and opinions to take into account. Will you be able to live with *yourself* as a writer of porn? I personally happen to think that most porn tends to devalue women; exploitation on a lot of levels is common in this genre. And as a feminist and a mother, I admit to at times wondering just what the hell I'm doing. I actually get a tremendous amount of enjoyment (not to mention a paycheck) writing for magazines that consistently give off negative attitudes and images of women. Or, if not negative, as least fairly skewed.

Do I want my daughter thinking that big breasts and a skinny waist are her ticket to the good life? (For now I'll just conveniently ignore the fact that those messages run rampant in the non-porn magazines as well.) Do I want her to think for one minute that she was put here on earth to do the kinds of things or behave in the ways that they show and tell in the magazines? Or, even if she does choose to do that, do I want her doing it in front of thousands or millions of people? Do I really ever want to see her in one of those magazines?

Do I want my son to have the distorted view that this is what regular/normal women do? Do I want him to think it's okay to think of women solely in terms of what they look like or what kind of sex they're willing/wanting to have? Do I want him to behave towards women the way some of the magazines advise?

Of course not. And when the time comes I'll talk to them about it...about the difference between fantasy and reality. About the difference between what people think about doing and what they actually do. About how it's ok to think about/want to do all kinds of things, it's just not always ok to do them.

Mostly I'll talk to them then, as I do now, about how, in the real world, men and women need to work on mutual respect and equality, in the bedroom as well as in the kitchen. After that, what you do in the privacy of either room is your business.

In the meantime I try to remember that the world of porn is a fantasy land. Having known enough men who actually buy and read porn on a regular basis, I've learned that they *know* it's not the real world. That's why they buy it. Why pay good money for more real world anyway? Even though most publications masquerade as real life, the people that buy them know better. They're looking for fantasies. Their own and mine. And, while we both may wonder at times where that line between fantasy and reality is drawn, and while it's my job as a writer to blur that line, to make my reader believe what I'm writing about is real, most people still know the difference.

Fantasy aside, though, porn can still be quite degrading to women. As if dealing with my own prejudices as well as other's weren't enough to scare me away from writing porn, there's always the fact that I regularly run smack dab into the whole issue of feminism, a club I am proud to claim membership in. Never one to apologize, I've always tried not to utter the dismissive phrase "I'm a feminist, but..."

In this context, though, it's sometimes hard not to. How can one be a feminist and even *read* this made-for-men smut, let alone write it? How can I - a woman who's very first adult statement to the world, in the form of a poster, was *Don't call me girl!* - write for magazines that insist on using that (and other even less flattering terms) exclusively? How can I refuse to use the word *girl* to describe *women* in this book and then proceed to blithely dismiss my own convictions in my work?

Dunno.

Really, I don't. The particular mix of feminism and porn is one I never did figure out. Not when I was nineteen and a fervent defender of women's rights and reader of porn. Not now that I'm a writer of porn and a mom and a wife in a very satisfying, equal partnership.

About all I can come up with is that as people, we all have the right to be who we are, especially as it pertains to our sexuality and our fantasies. If who we are includes unexplainable contradictions, so be it. I sure don't have any better answers and I've been working on it for years.

But sure, I still wonder.

Say, for example, I happen to be writing about two teenage lesbian lovers who take on a man just for fun. Now, I know full well that the likelihood of two *real* lesbians doing something like that are about as likely as winning the lottery. Probably less so. So am I doing myself, my audience, *anybody*, a disservice by pretending that this is real? Or is it ok, because it's my fantasy too, and fantasies are like feelings, they're ok as long as you don't act inappropriately on them?

Unfortunately, although I keep searching, I don't have answers for most of these questions. Some days I believe that I'm crazy to be writing this exploitative stuff. The next day I'm having too much fun writing my newest story to even think such negative thoughts. That's just the sometimes-twisted realities that I live with. Just like me, you'll have to come to terms with your own questions, your own answers, your own realities.

If your particular reality, like mine, includes the enjoyment of porn, maybe you don't need all the answers either. In the end, for reasons I don't fully understand, I *love* writing porn. I thoroughly enjoy fashioning stories about new and exciting ways and places to have wild sex. And I like to do twists on the old, boring ways also; to breathe new life into the missionary position, say, or add a spark to married, monogamous lovers. I love searching my own personal fantasy databases for inventive and often extreme ideas. I love challenging myself with my own beliefs or hang-ups or taboos. I sometimes find myself in the middle of a first draft, creating something new and different and feeling like the luckiest person in the world because I get to do this for a living.

And, in addition to enjoying the writing of porn, I also love reading it. Always have. Years ago, at the tender age of nineteen, I relished my dubious status as that of fledgling feminist who also happened to subscribe to Playboy and Penthouse. I thoroughly enjoyed reading the stories *and* looking at the pictures. Not that I could ever really explain it. No, I'm not gay. And yes, I know for a fact that most women don't look like that and don't need to, anyway.

But I still like it.

Porn is provocative. It intrigues and excites me. If it does that to you, if it stimulates *all* of your senses, chances are good that you'll be able to write it.

Personally, I believe that people enjoy reading what they would enjoy writing. What they are *able* to write. Not that we're always aware, as readers, of those tendencies. Twenty years ago, perusing my collection of dirty magazines, it never even occurred to me that I would ever try to *write* that stuff. Sure, I was a closet writer and had fantasies about my personal essays appearing in Woman's Day, another magazine that I read religiously. But porn? *Please!*

It wasn't until years later when I attempted my first few full-length porn stories, found them remarkably easy to craft, and then sold them easily and quickly for more money than I'd expected did I suddenly realize that I was, for whatever reason, able to do this thing. Able and willing to make money writing what I enjoyed reading. Wow, what a concept. One that can work for you.

Still don't know? Haven't read much porn? Start now. Go exploring in that adults-only room of your neighborhood newsstand. Peruse the magazines. Poke around back there and pick out three to six of them. Choose a few of the major ones, the ones you're more familiar with. Then be daring and check out some of the less mainstream ones, the ones with titles and pictures and stories you've only imagined. Now, take them home and read them cover-to-cover.

There now, did you enjoy that? If you did, you can probably write porn. It's really as simple as that. If reading all that smut embarrassed you and made you squirm, then this is probably not the forum for you. But if it intrigued you and set a fire under you, then that's all you need to know. If most of the words and pictures and innuendo didn't scare you (not too much anyway) then you're probably capable of using those same nasty words and ideas and concepts in your own stories.

Not that writing porn is never embarrassing or awkward; I'm *still* nervous about going into that little back room all by myself. It's not as though those guys back there, their faces buried behind opened magazines, really want some *real* woman intruding on their fantasy world. And I have to admit that sometimes I'm still shocked when I see my stories in print. I read through them and find myself cringing – did I really say that? Was that really little ol' me who used that filthy word or phrase? Little ol' suburban me who has fantasies and thoughts like *that*? I'm often amazed (after the fact) that these stories and kinks actually came from me.

At the time, during the creation and writing of the story, it feels natural. I feel good about my ability to read and target a market. I'm proud of being able to put together 3,000-word stories that have plot, dialogue, characterization and – oh, yeah, lots of hot sex. I also look forward to beginning work in the morning and I'm frustrated at 3 o'clock when I have to quit to go pick up the kids.

In general, I love what I write. That's the key. Do you like it? Do you *really* like it? All of the other details like controversy and feminism and what your mother will think should pale in relation to this simple fact: If you love it, you can do it.

Following Your Conscience

One of the reasons that porn has such a bad rap, deserved or not, is because of its extremes. Do much reading at all and you will find some pretty disgusting stuff out there. There's plenty of degradation to go around, and then some. I'm constantly amazed at how vile some magazine's content is. Amazed and occasionally dismayed - this is what I do for a living? Ok, so I don't actually write the really vile stuff. But writing smut is still my profession, and those extremes are part of it.

And I'm not even talking about the real extremes, say, the illegal writings. But even within the confines of the completely legal, there is still plenty to offend us all, especially those of us with a brain. There are really only a few magazines out there that for me, don't or haven't crossed any of my boundaries at all, the rest run the gamut from benign to purely ugly.

Of course, it's all relative – what offends me may not bother you at all. Taste is a rather subjective thing. And fickle, too, it can and does change to fit your age, mood and/or social status. There are things that didn't used to offend me but sure do now, and vice versa. I used to be outraged by the extreme poses of the models. Surely, I thought with disdain, we could leave something to the imagination. Now, however, I'm not only not offended, but I can occasionally even see art where I used to see only too-graphic posturing. And I sometimes find myself amused by un-politically-correct musings, depending on how close to home they hit. Of course I'm just as often completely dismayed by the rude and crude comments or attitudes in some of my favorite magazines, which is precisely my point. You never know what's going to offend you or someone else. All you can do is follow your own sometimes-contradictory conscience.

In order to write porn, you will, at some point, have to draw your own lines in the sand. Some of these may be obvious. Others can sometimes leave you wondering. For me, it ends up a balancing act, although occasionally it can feel more like a tightrope.

I knew from the beginning that I wouldn't do the obvious, no incest, underage, pain, or humiliation and degradation. But then after several years in the business I started writing for the "younger woman, older man" magazines. These are geared towards sometimes much older men who are interested in eighteen to twenty-two year-old women.

I quickly found my comfort zone within that genre, mainly that I didn't like to go above a certain age for the men in my stories. Mid-thirties I could deal with. Forties and up I decided to forego. It just didn't feel comfortable. That particular boundary works fine for me and I haven't had any trouble getting work given those limitations. But there can still be conflict.

Like, will I still feel as comfortable doing these sweet-young-thing stories as my daughter approaches and goes beyond puberty? Will I be less likely to want to write about teenage virgins as she grows up and I see real-live grown men looking at her? I have to look at the possibility that my boundaries and tolerances may change. In the meantime, that "innocent young woman" slant can already, at times, take me uncomfortably close to an exploitative edge. I have to be careful to not be led where I don't want to go.

For example, one editor asked me to do a piece on how to dump a young girlfriend. *Be brutal*, she said, *give examples of how, if the girl doesn't do this or that right, you get rid of her*. It would have been a fairly quick couple hundred dollars. Now I know there are plenty of people, professionals that I know and respect, who wouldn't have had any trouble with this article. But I just couldn't feel good

about it, especially given the tender young age range of the intended
dump-ee. So even though I'd always done articles the way this editor
wanted me to, I finally had to turn this one down.

It was the first and only time I'd turned down a story, and it
was a surprisingly hard thing for me to do. I was very concerned
that my decision would compromise my future relationship with
this editor. In the end, it was a chance I had to take. Luckily, there
were no negative consequences, and I was able to feel positive about
the whole situation because I hadn't sunk to a level that made me
uncomfortable.

Those levels are not always clear, though. Ok, I don't do
degradation or humiliation. That's easy enough. But how about a
little light female dominance? With the woman in charge? There's
always some level of humiliation in those stories, even if ever-so-
slight, even if only in the participant's mind.

Or what about spanking or water sports or leg sex or smoking,
all genres that can include at least obsession if not out-and-out
dominance? I love writing in all of those genres *because* of their
obsessive nature, because as a writer I get to stretch and dabble in
areas heretofore unfamiliar to me. But I don't like degradation and
humiliation. Where does that fit in my nice, neat little "lines in the
sand" scenario? Are these subjects going to have to be off limits for
me or can I find some happy medium?

Often you can. My answer to this particular problem, how to
approach subjects like humiliation without selling myself out or
feeling uncomfortable, was fairly easy. Any of my really obsessive
stories (which are truly the most fun to write) have a conflicted
narrator at their heart, one who's dealing with his own sexual
shame issues but usually within his own head. He's almost always
voyeuristic, that way I don't end up writing about actual humiliation,
of or by my main characters. I just get deep inside my character's

head and let his obsessive and demented tendencies get the best of him.

Another option is to pick your markets wisely. Even within the more extreme fetish subjects there are usually plenty of magazines within each category to choose from. And each one is going to have a different slant. Some are seriously hardcore, some just play at it. Some magazines in the leg sex category go all out, they contain serious humiliation and extreme degradation. On the other hand, some magazines don't want that at all, they go for the softer, obsessed yet still respectful angle. You're sure to be able to find magazines that fit your comfort zone.

When writing about sex, just as when actually doing it, comfort matters. Don't be afraid to go down paths you've never been down before, but don't feel that you need to force yourself into uncomfortable situations either.

Tools Of The Trade

So, what does it actually take to be a practicing porn writer aside from the relatively obvious; good writing skills, an open and imaginative mind, and a low embarrassment threshold?

Do you need editorial connections, a state of the art computer with accompanying designer software, and the latest copier and fax machine?

Nah.

The actual physical props you need to get started, the tools of this trade, are amazingly few.

For those of you who might be tempted to give excuses as to why you can't possibly be a writer *until* (insert excuse here), you're out of luck. Technically, (and especially if you're a really good typist or just have plenty of time on your hands) you could get by with just a typewriter and access to a neighborhood copy machine.

Years ago I sold my very first letters for a whopping $5.00 each using only a manual typewriter and plenty of correction tape. I won't pretend it was easy and I've tried to erase from my memory the agony of trying so hard to get it right that my fingers would sweat on the keys, only to have to redo an entire page because of one stupid un-fixable mistake. And I also am extremely aware of how easy I have it now with my computer in terms of text manipulation and rewrites. But, even in these technological times, it is possible to actually put out stories with very minimal equipment.

Of course, for ease of manuscript preparation and record

keeping, the following two items can be worth their weight in gold.

- **Computer**
- **Laser Printer**

But that's it. No, really, that's all you absolutely have to have, at least in the beginning. After you begin to sell, or even when you're just putting out a fair number of manuscripts, there are a few items that can make your life a little easier. A **phone line** and a **modem**, along with an **e-mail account**, come in handy for those editors who accept communication that way. I've found e-mail to be a fantastic way to communicate with editors that I already have a relationship with. Be careful of this mode of communication, though. Save it until you've already been introduced to an editor through more traditional means.

I've forged several strong working relationships with editors via e-mail, mostly owing to its speedy and personal nature. E-mail has been a life (or at least job) saver in several instances, sparing both editors and me catastrophic late deadlines by a timely transmission of last minute e-mails. (And of course, for those editors who prefer their submissions by e-mail, freeing me from the tedious process of sending out manuscripts via snail-mail, I reserve my undying gratitude.)

Some sort of **fax machine** capability may prove to be of benefit, since many editors prefer to fax contracts and guidelines rather then send them via snail-mail or e-mail. Also, when you're on the phone with a hurried editor, it's awkward and hardly professional to be fumbling through the phone book trying to look up the number for the nearest accept-a-fax store. Then there's the wasted time and money spent driving to retrieve or send said fax to consider.

Luckily I've found an alternative to the traditional fax machine, one that's worked fine for my limited needs. There are companies that, for free, will allow you to receive faxes via e-mail. The faxes are sent to you in the normal way, that is, the sender dials up your personal fax number, but you receive them as an e-mail document. For a very reasonable fee, these companies will also give you other options, such as a local number, or a toll-free number and can also be configured to send faxes from your e-mail. All in all, this is a truly viable alternative to an expensive and bulky fax machine.

One thing I don't have yet – but that is quite high on my wish list - is a **scanner.** There's no better way to send photos and, lacking a copier, a scanner can also come in handy for e-mailing documents and contracts and such. While I haven't encountered too many editors who have expected or asked for this kind of communication, there have been a few. And, while my last experience at the neighborhood copy store - scanning and storing dozens of photos to send to an editor as aids to his illustrator - was relatively hassle free, it would have been easier to do all that work from the comfort of my own desk.

Of course, there are basic office supplies, some optional, some required: A filing cabinet or two and a comfortable chair are helpful. A box of 9 x 12 clasp envelopes and a ream or two of decent quality paper are more or less necessary. Also you'll need plenty of #10 envelopes, paper clips, and labels, along with the requisite hundred or so stamps at the ready.

Other than that, to successfully write porn, you don't need an office, you don't need a business account, and you don't even need letterhead or business cards.

For years I wrote in a tiny little corner of my mostly-finished basement. Sure, it was cold, somewhat stifling, and of course fairly dark. The dimness finally drove me to distraction, especially on beautiful spring days. So I relocated. Now I write upstairs in a slightly larger corner of my living room instead. Yeah, I'd love a bigger and better space. I have dreams about an addition that would house not only a master bedroom and laundry room, but a bright corner office next to the lilac bushes where I could fantasize in relative and well-lit peace. In the meantime, however, I'm fairly content in my living room. At least it's *close* to a window, not to mention the refrigerator and the coffee maker. While I'd certainly like a change of venue, to successfully write porn, I don't need one. And neither do you.

You do, however, need drive, some basic common sense, and good, solid business skills.

Taking Care Of Business

Whatever form your writing takes, whether porn or poetry or mainstream articles, taking care of the business end of it should be top priority. While good writing is, of course, of utmost importance, professionalism is also a must in this business. Editors, even at the smaller publications, receive far too many submissions to even begin to consider the less than professional ones. You must take yourself and your job seriously if you expect an editor to do the same.

Some basics of my own business strategies:

I use a general filing system for most of my paperwork (that is, when it's not strewn about on the desk and floor). I've got folders for just about everything.

• The most important file holds the writers' guidelines that I religiously send away for and I'm amazed at how often I peruse this particular file. It might be that I'm in the middle of an article or story and need to check on a word limit. Or maybe I need to find out who handles the submissions so I know where to aim my query.

Occasionally I'll go through this file for ideas or to see which ones are out of date and need to be replaced. (Date them when you receive them otherwise you'll never know how old they are.) Quite often, in rereading an editor's guidelines, I'll find something I've missed, some obvious bit of information that can make the difference between a sale and a rejection.

• I put all of my rejections and acceptances, along with any extra copies of contracts, into one folder. (As one could expect, this file is fairly fat by now. Like any good writer, I'm sure I could paper at least one wall with the rejections alone. Luckily I'm too busy writing to spare any time on that endeavor.) This file comes in handy when double-checking rights that I've sold to see whether I can re-sell a piece or when trying to revise a story based on an editor's feedback.

■I have a file for receipts even though my expenses are relatively few and far between. And I have one for extra hard copies of stories, although I don't often re-use my rejected submissions, preferring to use a fresh copy instead. I also have an idea folder and one that lists all of past, current and potential markets. These don't get used as often, but I'll sometimes find that perfect idea or market that I stashed away last year and promptly forgot about.

■I also have a shelf filled with books to help me out. Valerie Kelly's old *How to Write Erotica* is what helped me get started years ago. Plus I have the requisite Dictionaries, a Thesaurus and a Style Manual. I've got some general writing guides and market guides galore, although the market listings for porn are woefully inadequate.

■And then, of course, there's the shelf filled with magazines. Ah, my greatest asset – my collection of dirty magazines! I have one of everything and then some. My collection is absolutely invaluable. I strongly suggest that you build up one of your own. As a matter of fact, I can't see succeeding in this genre unless you do. Yes, it's expensive, but ultimately it's your most precious resource. I can't even begin to guess at the number of times I thumb through them in any given week – checking out editors' names, or style and slant changes. I quite often catch something that I'd missed before, something that triggers just the right story idea. From inspiration to hard facts to advertising angles, my magazines hold almost everything I need.

■I also have a large database of **computerized files**. Lists of markets and their needs. Lists of ideas. "To-do" lists that I update regularly. All of my stories, categorized of course, along with some half finished stories that were rejected but that I can't bear to send to the recycle bin.

I have a business file where I keep track of my submissions, queries and contacts. I can go back and tell you how long it's been since I sent which story to which market, when it was accepted, what the terms were, and when I got paid. I can tell you when I'm supposed to get paid and how much. Busy work, it sometimes feels like, but very important to my success as a writer.

Without my humongous business file I'd be lost. It's imperative that I know which markets I'm selling to and which ones never respond. And I need to know when a magazine usually does respond but didn't this time, indicating that I need to send out another copy of the story. I like to know which markets I should write off completely and which ones are still offering even a glimmer of hope. I can also track my percentages and find out how much of my work is selling.

Sometimes, due to particularly sluggish editor response or editorial changes, I need to re-think my submission strategy. And sometimes, due to factors largely out of my control, I need to rethink my writing strategy to focus on other angles or markets.

Of course I also have a copy of every single story I've ever written saved on a disk. Sooner rather than later, I mean to back it all up on hard copy, too, since just this morning I had a corrupted disk (of a one-of-a-kind five-year-old first draft, of course) that wouldn't open all the way. Sure it's time consuming, not to mention rather confusing. I have lots of disks. But do I need to tell you to back up your computer files? Do I need to tell you to back them up *every single day*? Do I need to tell you about the heartache of a hard drive crash?

Just imagine that every thing you've ever written is trashed, every single idea and inspiration - not to mention the next Great American Porn novel - is lost forever. Imagine that it's completely irretrievable. Not a pretty picture, is it?

Don't chance it. Back up your files onto disks and/or hard copy, *always.*

Taxes – The ultimate sign of your success

There'll come a time in your career as a porn writer where you will begin to actually receive money for your work and it will be a glorious day indeed. Well, except for that fateful day when your taxes come due, of course. Then it can seem that you hardly get to keep any of that hard earned money at all. Painful though it is, paying taxes on your income is one of those necessary little evils of freelancing.

If you already have some experience with being self-employed, you'll know the drill, but if not, here are the bare-bones basics.

Not being an expert on the subject, I won't go into too much detail about all the various things you can deduct or loopholes you can look for, but there are plenty of experts and publications that will. In general, though, paying self-employment taxes is a fairly easy procedure. If I can figure it out, you can, too.

Any reputable magazine will send you a form at the beginning of the calendar year. Similar to the familiar W-2 that you receive from your employer, this one is called a 1099. It lists all the monies that this particular publication paid out to you in the previous year. Simply put, you'll take this total, deduct what you can and then add it to any of your other income to give you a grand total.

There are only two forms that you'll need. Net Profit From Business (Schedule C-EZ) on which you'll figure your expenses and your net profit. (You are tracking them all, right? From mileage and car expenses to printer cartridges to long distance charges, you of course need to make sure you document anything related to your writing career). Armed with this information (your net profit), you'll proceed to the Self Employment Tax Form (Schedule SE, form 1040).This simple form will let you figure you how much you owe on your writing income.

So now you have both your net earnings and your self-employment tax figured. Take the earnings and add them to any other wages on your 1040 (not the 1040a, you can't do the short form if using self-employment income on your return). Then add your self employment taxes to the Other Tax part of your return and voila, you're done.

Well, except for the paying part.

These two forms are usually all that are necessary if your total earnings are less than something like $68,000. It's a rather simple, albeit painful part of the writing life to have to part with your hard earned money this way. But I look at it as a necessary price to pay for the privilege of doing what I enjoy for a living!

Choosing Your Pseudonym

Do you have to use a pseudonym? No, not really. You could certainly choose to write under your own name. Plenty of porn authors, from writers of literary erotica to editors of major porn magazines, do. Some don't have any problem at all using their given name, they're proud of what they do and not ashamed to show it.

Most writers of porn, though, choose fictitious monikers for a variety of reasons. There's the parent of three who'd rather that the other preschool dads not know what he does in his spare time. Or the businesswoman who doesn't want her boss to know that he's jerking off to a story written by his underling. There are the shy types who'd be embarrassed to have anyone know what they do (or fantasize about doing) behind closed doors. Or, more simply, there are those people that accept porn's controversial nature and are just not comfortable 'outing' themselves.

Whatever the reason, if you do decide to use a pseudonym, have fun picking your name. Even though you could certainly use a different name each time, inventing your own marketable image can give you an edge as a writer. I like to think that it fosters reader identification. In this faceless, nameless world of porn, seeing a familiar name on a story can matter.

Familiar is good, stupid is not. I'm not very fond of the obvious ones: Peter Hardd, Suzie Sleaze, Dick or Kitty *anything*. True, for some venues, especially those that manage to successfully spoof themselves, fun and outrageous names can work. But for all the others, stick to the simple. When I read porn I like to know that the author is not talking down to me, and a silly name smacks a little of sarcasm. But if that's your style – irreverent humor, say – by all means, pick something that indicates that. Choose a name that mirrors your style and projects the image you want to create.

Creating that other persona for yourself is part of the fun. Personally I think of Katy (you didn't think that was my real name, now did you?!) as my alter ego, or, rather, several of my alter egos. All of which include me on some level but are still separate. I love thinking of Katy as a distinct identity. It gives me a completely different self than my outward suburban one to play with. Besides, s*he* writes these things, not me!

There are writers who use several different pseudonyms; one for the lesbian confession, one for the hard-hearted womanizer, still another for the persecuted fetishist. I have one I use for some of the stories I write from a man's perspective.

Not all magazines will let you use your pseudonym, of course. Those that buy all rights will often choose a name for you. And not all stories have bylines, either. That true-life confession signed by "Anonymous" certainly isn't going to have your name under the titillating title. It pays to check the magazine first and then submit your piece with bylines in mind. If you do use a pseudonym, type it directly under your story title. But in addition to your pseudonym, you must also put your real name and address on your manuscripts. Editors obviously need to know what name to put on the check.

In the beginning of my career, it made me more than just a little nervous sending out stories with my pseudonym *and* my real name on them. Over time, and after dealing with plenty of professional and conscientious editors, I became more confident. Of course, then there was the day, just last month, when I opened up a copy of a magazine to see not only the title of my story, but my *real* name printed there as well. And no, I wasn't looking at an artsy little story, one that I could perhaps call erotica. No, this one, with my *very* unique name printed under it...this one was pure sleaze.

Seems that the pseudonym got lost in the transfer between the new editor and the old one. After extreme embarrassment and much fretting over who might actually see it (my ex-husband?, my child's science teacher?) I finally reassured myself with the rather lame notion that anyone reading a magazine about how to have sex with 19-year-olds may have more reason than I do to stay underground.

So yes, I hate to be the bearer of bad news, but it does happen. If you're going to write this stuff, sooner or later you very well might be 'outed' against your will. Can a porn writer ever be completely anonymous? I doubt it. There's always that chance that someone you don't want to find out, will. In my case I've just had to accept that as a part of the risks of writing porn, of which there are relatively few, and try not to take it too seriously.

II
Before You Begin

Ok, so you've decided that you want to be a porn writer when you grow up. Yessirree, Bub, this is obviously the profession for you.

You've got your computer running, your files ready for that first acceptance letter, your envelopes bought and your inhibitions lowered.

Now what?

Well, unlike when we were back in school, now comes the fun part....

Doing Your Homework

I consider this part of writing porn, doing my homework, to be one of the best perks of writing porn. At it's most basic, I get to sit around the house in the middle of the day while the kids are in school and pore over dirty magazines. Ok, so maybe it's not just porn writers that do this kind of thing. There are plenty of just plain...um...perverts sitting around doing the exact same thing. But at my house, we call it *research*. And I honestly try to give it the respect it deserves.

Fun though it may be, there's quite an art to researching markets. It requires a lot of time and a fair amount of critical thinking. You have to get past the stories and articles and pictures, which are what the editor wants you as a reader to see, and ferret out what the editor doesn't necessarily want you to see. Which is that, as an editor, he knows exactly who you, as a reader, are, and what your likes and dislikes are, and is only too happy to feed them up to you, in the proper proportions, month after month.

And it's precisely this, figuring out a magazine's readership (and thus it's editorial needs), that's the most crucial element to targeting your stories to the right editors. Without this. you will not succeed. It's really as simple as that. If you're not paying attention and writing to the right markets, you're not going to sell. Sex magazines are very specific, very narrowly focused. They have their readership pegged, and you need to arm yourself with this knowledge, too, in order to sell to them. When you're reading to ascertain a magazine's market, really try to get inside the reader's head.

For example, after picking up the latest issue of a fairly mainstream magazine I was able to say with a relative degree of certainty that this market likes...

• Anal sex, but only on the sly, because it's really just a fantasy and they sure don't do this with their wives or girlfriends. And they're mostly in the 30-50 year old range and married or in committed relationships. They are professionals in the $30,000-and-up category with working significant others. Yes, there also may be some blue collar workers among the lot, but it's still their goal to work up to management. And they don't like anything even remotely smacking of gay sex, but they sure like their lesbian threesomes, preferably with said wife or girlfriend and her best friend. They like their women on the slim side, with shaved genitals and smaller-sized, more natural-looking breasts. And they like them smart and professional, or at least   semi-savvy and never brainless. They enjoy relatively equal relationships with their women, so there'll be no degradation or derision in the stories. But there can be a fair amount of humor. And they don't like the women terribly young. They're usually at least 22 and can go up as high as a very healthy and toned 45.

• From a critical read through of their editorial content I also see that they're not running full length erotica, but they do run two shorter pieces per month, perhaps around 2,000 words. I make a note of the titles of these regular features and see that they're both written from the man's perspective; a rather well-spoken, fairly highly educated man at that. No street talk here. Plenty of hard-core sex, though, just couched in slightly more genteel tones than some other magazines.

• Their non-fiction is more of the hard news variety; a celebrity interview, an article on men and their toys, a selection of hot vacation spots. No fluff fiction posing as non-fiction here, or at least if it is, it's well camouflaged.

• There are, however, plenty of letters that look fairly contrived, probably staff written. Some of the verbiage is the same from letter to letter and they're a little too standardized to be coming from the average reader. They run about 600 words and each one concerns one of the scenarios mentioned above; wife and girlfriend, anal sex with wife, etc.

• So, while I'll still need to send away for the writer's guidelines on this one (I'll need to know exact word lengths as well as which editor to submit to and what their current needs are), it looks like the easiest way to break into this particular market is with shorter fiction and letters to the editor.

All this from just a read-through or two. Well, okay, an incredibly thorough read-through. And that was just once. I don't feel as though I've fully absorbed a magazine until I've read at *least* two issues cover to cover. From the masthead and editorial office address (it helps to know who you're dealing with and if there are any changes month to month) to the letters to the editor (staff written? reader written? any specific slant or style?) to the captions under the photos (does the magazine freelance this work out also?) to the stories (word length, tone, style), to the phone sex ads in the back (you'll find out a lot about who a particular magazine is targeting by carefully studying their ads).

You'll pick up an amazing amount of information about a magazine's target market (and hence their editorial needs) from these in-depth readings. After you combine this with the specifications from their writer's guidelines, you'll end up with a very good feel for your market's likes and dislikes, which is essential if you're going to be writing for them.

Pay close attention to a market's competition also, and you'll glean even more from your readings. Which markets compete and how do they differ? For example, there are literally dozens of "younger woman/older man" magazines out there, and they all have a slightly different slant. Some go for the "bad" girl aspect, some present only "good" girls. Some are more explicit in their pictorials and their stories. Some like their women coy, some like them savvy. Some are geared toward men in their 20s, some toward men in their 50s and 60s. Some emphasize college, some feel that college has been done to death and refuse any stories of school at all. Some have full-length fiction, some only have stories in the 1200-1500 word range. Some don't have any fiction at all, but do have letters or columns or bits of news information. Some only have first person accounts of wild sexual exploits, supposedly written by their readers and some have advice columns or a regular columnist. Pay attention to a market that appears to do the opposite of their competition. You may be able to write so as to highlight their differences.

The more you can learn about your targeted markets, the better. An editor wants you to know what her magazine is like before you submit to it. She's going to be quite annoyed while reading the umpteenth manuscript (yours) about a trash-talking, nude-dancing 19-year-old when her magazine, striving to best the competition who features just that, focuses more on the virginal and shy sorority girl.

While these very tightly focused markets can sometimes work in your favor, giving you more markets to send to, it can also be more limiting as far as sales are concerned. The story that you tailor specifically toward one market often won't sell in another similar market without a major rewrite. It can be frustrating to write specifically to a market only to be rejected because they have a backlog of stories. Then you're stuck with having to, say, trim 1,000 words off your masterpiece *and* change the point of view in order to get another market to even look at it.

But on a positive note, the more you do your homework and refine your market search, the more you'll sell. And once your stories are selling, you'll be dealing directly with editors. Editors who know that you're able to write to their market will be only too happy to give you work and ignore the building slush-pile of manuscripts from writers who haven't been paying attention.

Keep in mind that while some markets obviously suggest their own subject, never deviating from their slant – and you are wise to stick within those guidelines – occasionally it can pay to challenge that. One market I've sold to is very rigid in their guidelines and fairly set in their ways. They don't experiment much. They like their characters fairly boring, fairly ordinary.

On a whim, I sent in a rather experimental piece. I definitely considered this story *cutting edge* for this particular market. Surprisingly enough, they bought it, although the editor and I both agreed that it was quite a departure from their tried-and-true way.

Of course then there are the markets that never deviate. One market I've dealt with is also quite rigid, they're very couple oriented and category specific. While you can play around a little with plots and scenarios, this market definitely has a plan as far as sex and characters. Once I'd finally figured out their formula and sold several stories to them I decided that I, personally, really didn't want to write for a market that was so specific. But that kind of format and structure can work for a lot of writers.

While not nearly as fun as the reading part of *Doing Your Homework,* sending away for writer's guidelines is, nonetheless, a mandatory part of the process.

Most magazines that accept freelance work put out guidelines that tell prospective submitters what their needs are and how and to whom to submit. While they're not often completely accurate (editors and policies change faster than the guidelines, it seems), they are an invaluable tool for the porn writer.

Combined with the read-through of your chosen magazine, the writer's guidelines should give you all the information you need to submit. They will tell you word counts and let you know whether or not you have to query first. Almost invariably they'll stress that you need to be familiar with their magazine before you submit.

Often they'll tell you which editor is in charge of submissions as well as remind you that an SASE is mandatory.

Editors often expect that you will have studied the guidelines before you submit and will not take kindly to submissions that don't fit their criteria.

To send away for a market's guidelines, simply send them a letter (along with a #10 SASE) politely asking for a copy of the writer's guidelines. Yes, there will be plenty of magazines that never respond and your stamp will be wasted but, in the end, that fat file of guidelines that you do receive will help you sell enough stories to make up for them!

The Magazine Formats:
Letters, short stories and non-fiction

In your readings, you will by now have found that there are three main text formats found in magazine porn: letters, short stories, and non-fiction. While there are others - such as regular columns, writing for copy and "confessions" - the three basic formats are the most open to freelancers and where you'll get the majority of your work.

Letters

Often the easiest of the magazine markets to break into, hence great for beginning porn writers, letters have their downside as well. Whether staff written, reader written or professional-writer written (and often it's difficult to tell), most magazines don't pay much for them, if at all. There are exceptions, of course, and once you're more established it's possible to find markets for letters that pay quite well. In the beginning, however, you're probably going to be stuck on the low end of the pay scale. But even if there's no money involved at all, letters can be great practice when you're beginning.

By starting small, with letters instead of longer stories, you can practice refining your technique within a structure. Don't just practice them at home, though, and then move on to the good stuff. *You* may think they're good enough to appear in your targeted magazine, but an editor may not, and it's important that you have an accurate gauge of your skill level before you try your hand at the harder markets.

So if the magazine solicits for reader written letters, go ahead and study the format and see if you can put together a few of your own. Do a rough word count of the letters in the magazine you're targeting and stick to that. The more common word lengths for letters are between 600 and 800 words although they can occasionally run as high as 1200 or so words.

Once you have a few acceptances for free letters under your belt, you can move onto the next stage and target the paid letters market as well as the short story market. (See Chapter IV – Story Specifics - for more on letter writing.)

Short Stories

Short fiction is my favorite kind of porn to both read *and* write. Obviously there's more room within the story to move around, more character development, more plot, and, of course much more sex than in a smaller sized letter. The average story is around 3,000 words, which translates to about 10 pages, although it varies from magazine to magazine. Other common lengths are 1,500 words and 2,000 words.

Keep in mind that most magazines are quite specific about their word lengths and often won't even read anything that's not within their range. For example, I tried and tried to get writer's guidelines for a particular market, but to no avail. Finally I sent them my best attempt at a 3,000 word story geared right to them, only to have it sent back with a hand written comment saying that they only accepted stories that were 2500 words in length and, since mine didn't qualify, it was being returned unread.

It seemed rather persnickety to me at the time. After all, I certainly could have cut the length if they'd liked the style. But since word length does have a great deal to do with how the story is set up, it must not have been worth this editor's time to even check. The 3,000-word story, for instance, most often has two sex scenes; one set up by at least the third page and lasting about 2 pages, the second one beginning less than a page after the first and lasting at least 3 pages. A 1,500 or 2,000-word story, however, often has just one sex scene that starts sooner (perhaps the first or second page) and usually continues throughout the entire story. The shorter piece is often a little faster paced which is sometimes better for magazines that focus a lot on pictorials.

It takes a fair amount of practice to put these stories together in a way that fits the format. But if you've been reading enough of them, you will have absorbed some of it by simple osmosis. Without even realizing it you may already know when a story doesn't quite fit, you may find yourself bogged down in detail, hurrying to 'get to the good part' or scanning back wondering how the heck the plot moved there. By paying attention now to the structure, you'll be able to piece it all together, and your stories will begin to flow. (See Chapter IV – Story Specifics – for more information on short story writing.)

Non-fiction

Non-fiction is much harder to break into than fiction. While most porn editors will accept unsolicited manuscripts for fiction, they'll still require a query for nonfiction. And since they often like to work with more experienced writers for articles, your query is likely to be ignored in favor of the authors they already know, leaving you, the unknown, in the dust.

A way around this is to become one of an editor's *known* writers. In my experience that's the key to being able to write nonfiction for magazines – getting to know the editor. Eventually, as he/she gets a feel for your writing, you will probably be offered something. Or at least you'll be in a better place to suggest an article idea yourself.

Non-fiction for porn comes in many flavors. There are interviews, celebrity profiles or exposes, how-to articles, product reviews, etc. There are editors who ask for documentation as to facts and figures, and there are editors who will assume that you're going to make up quotes and statistics. Word lengths vary widely, from 200 word fillers to 5000 word features.

Each magazine is different and each has different needs. Again, analyze your markets carefully. Study their articles, get a clue for what they buy, and always abide by their writers' guidelines. If you're interested in writing non-fiction, pay attention to the details just as you would for fiction. Find out which magazines use what word lengths and styles and then don't stray far from that format when querying or submitting. (See Chapter VI – Story Specifics – for more information on non-fiction writing.)

Some Additional Markets

There are plenty of venues for porn writing, although they can be somewhat difficult to find and contact. And once contacted, some are fairly closed to newcomers. I started with magazines because, at the time, they were the easiest to break into, but there are several more options to choose from.

Books

Check any major bookstore (especially the independents) and you should be able to find an Erotica section. (Also try the Sex section or Women's section). You'll find a wide variety of titles there, from the old Victorian classics, usually by "Anonymous", to some of the newer series titles. There are collections of short stories as well as themed fiction, which is similar to romance in its structure. There are books and collections geared solely toward women writers of porn and there are compilations of stories previously published by some of the bigger magazines.

The more mainstream romance-type porn is also starting to turn up at neighborhood newsstands. The store near me just recently added a whole shelf of them. These novels and story collections are quite likely to have a very detailed structure and you'll need to be well versed in their needs to be able to sell for them. That's where the writer's guidelines will again come in handy, write to each publisher and ask for a copy, then you'll have a starting place for your submissions.

Most of these books are not as open to beginners as other markets. The quality of writing is usually high and the competition fierce. But as you gain skill in the other markets, it may be worth your while to look into this one. The 'doing your homework' angle works for these publications as well. Study their formats, styles and guidelines carefully before you submit.

The Internet

With the advent of the Internet, a porn writer's chances of being published increased dramatically. For some writers, it's the only place they've seen their stories in print. As such, it can be a great tool for more traditional publishing as well as self-publishing.

But beware, it's also a medium that's been overused and there is a huge glut of porn out there, visual as well as written. Anybody can put their stories out there on the Internet; they can and they do.

In my own perusing of the Internet (specifically looking for porn stories and markets), I've found that story sites abound but they're mostly just thinly veiled advertisements for visual porn. And I've been quite disappointed by the quality of the writing at the legitimate (usually free) fiction sites. It's enough to make a decent porn writer cover her face in shame. There is some truly awful writing out there. From bad grammar to bad punctuation and bad plot, the Internet is definitely a Mecca for the amateur porn writer.

Erotica as a genre seems to fare somewhat a little better on the 'Net. There are actually a few decent sites with some fairly good literary erotica. The market hasn't quite caught up with itself yet, though, so beware. There are plenty of misleading sites out there.

There are also some decent 'zines and other sites out there that seem to be trying hard to get higher quality erotica into the mainstream. These sites are often 'labors of love' and as such don't tend to pay much or anything at all, but they can often work for the fledging porn writer. Editors here may be more willing to work with a writer that they like and are able to give critical feedback to.

Never trust anyone that offers to 'publish' your work for a fee. No matter how attractive these offers may seem, I have yet to run into a legitimate one. Your goal is to write what you love and get paid for it, remember? Don't believe anyone that says that 'paying your dues' includes paying them to publish your work.

One way to get your work out there is to work with an e-publisher, someone who will put your books or stories into virtual print and then either sell them for you or help you sell them yourself. My suggestion, if you want to explore this avenue, is to go with one who's well established. And I'd suggest that you beware of signing anything that takes away any of your electronic publishing rights if you want to be able to use your material again yourself.

Obviously, given the amount of sex for sale on and off the Web, there are many opportunities. There are markets for everything from phone sex scripts to scripts for audio sex tapes. Unfortunately, these markets can be quite difficult to find, but some serious surfing might lead you to viable venues.

Manuscript and Query Basics

When you're dealing in the written word, even in these increasingly automated times, your first contact with an editor is almost always visual. Whatever form your submission takes, the very first thing an editor sees is the presentation of your manuscript. It's crucial that this presentation be as professional as possible. Certainly there are plenty of great looking manuscripts that get rejected, but there are certainly many more *non-professional* looking manuscripts that don't even get read.

Make your first impression count!

While manuscript formats may vary, there are still some simple basic steps you can follow to make sure that your submissions are professional.

• Always buy decent quality printer, typing, or copy paper. Editors are going to notice when the paper they're holding is so cheap they can see through it. On the other hand, thicker, more pretentious paper isn't going to help your cause, either. Stick to the plain stuff. 20 or 24 pound is good. Most places sell 'multiuse' or 'multipurpose' paper, and then there's still the regular old "typing paper" from the grocery store that will work in a pinch.

• Keep your printer heads clean. Most printers will do this automatically. Just follow the directions on the machine. As soon as you spot a tell tale smudge, redo it. Smudges always look sloppy, even just little ones, even when there's only one, even if it's only on the envelope. (After all, the envelope actually precedes your manuscript as far as first impressions go.) And the same goes for typos; always redo them. Make it your goal to never send out a manuscript with an error.

Often, it can seem like a waste of time, money and energy to reprint entire pages or envelopes for just one small glitch. But remember that these editors don't know you. They have absolutely no reason to like you or to think that you are anything other than some pitiful wannabe who thinks s/he can write. Don't prove it with unprofessional, unclean copies.

Luckily, there are a few ways to save costs, although I've learned the hard way that you need to be careful when cutting corners.

After using generic ink cartridges exclusively for a few months the heads on my printer became clogged. It took a lot of electronic as well as manual cleaning to get the printer to work again. It's never been quite the same since.

But other generic supplies can work just fine. I used to buy my large mailing envelopes at the grocery store and lamented long and loud about how expensive it was to send out submissions. Of course, that was until I discovered office supply stores where I could buy 9x12 envelopes and #10 envelopes in bulk. If the post office ever decides to provide discounts on stamps in bulk, I'll be in heaven.

• Always use a fresh envelope, and always laser print the names and addresses onto it. If your 9 x 12s are too bulky for your printer, generate a computer printed label to put on the actual envelope. I'll occasionally hand letter things like copies of contracts that I'm sending back to an editor, but only after I have a good working relationship with him or her. And please, no colored envelopes. No bright, neon eye-catching hues. If you think that will get your submission noticed sooner, you're wrong. It will be one of the first to get tossed into the trash can.

• Use 12 or 14 point size for your font, *never* 10; you don't want to be blamed for the editor's ensuing eyestrain or migraine. Use

Times New Roman (in black) for your font. Again, anything catchy is not going to look professional.

• Always double check the spelling of your editor's name and always call ahead to make sure that s/he is still the one taking submissions.

• If you want a response to your manuscript (and who doesn't) enclose an SASE. I've had editors hand letter annoyed little comments on my returned goods on the few occasions that I've forgotten this rule. You can enclose a full 9 x 12 if you like but I use a #10 envelope, stamped of course, for the editor's response. It's a lot cheaper for me to simply reprint a rejected manuscript than to pay for its postage all the way back home. (An aside - What happens to all those SASE's floating around? Since most editors will use their own letterhead to send an acceptance letter, what on earth do they do with all those stamped envelopes I've sent out? Do they get reused? Are editors' trash cans brimming with unused stamps? Do they end up in a landfill? And what about all the times that my submissions, SASE and all, have been ignored? What then? Do they reuse *my* stamps for other writers' acceptances?)

• For the actual manuscript itself, formats vary. I've adapted my style over the years and now use one that works for me. I put my real name and contact information in the top left corner of my first manuscript page. That includes my name, address, phone number, fax and e-mail address. Then I put the title of the piece about halfway down this page, with my pseudonym directly under it. (If this is a submission for a piece that doesn't use a name or a pseudonym, don't put anything here.) I usually put the word count on the right hand side, halfway between the contact info and the title. On every page after that I put my real last name, followed by a dash and the page number, in the top right corner.

Sample First Page:

Hopeful Author
12 Lover's Lane
Suburbia, TX 77777
P(555) 555-5555
F(555) 555-5555
pornauthor@whatever.com

2,955 words

Catchy Title
By Pseudonym

Story begins...

Cover Letters

Your cover letter is simply a page that you send along with your manuscript, sometimes to impart more information about yourself, sometimes just to let the editor know what he is about to read and why. Not all editors require cover letters and not all editors even like them, but always use one if you're not sure. Keep your cover letters brief and to the point. Most editors of porn magazines are simply not interested in your credentials unless you're querying. When sending a complete manuscript, brevity is best. An editor is looking for a good, clean copy of a story that can stand on its own. Your story is going to need to sell itself. If it can't do that already, you need to rework it.

In the cover letter itself your editor will want contact information, story title, word count and not much else. Occasionally, you may need more information. If you've talked to the editor, for example, and he's asked for this particular piece, you may want to refresh his memory. Or if you're sending a simultaneous submission, you'll need to let him know. In general, the shorter the better.

Sample Cover Letter

Date

Porn Editor (be sure to use the actual name of the person if you can)
Porn Magazine
123 Erotica Dr.
Wild Nights, FL 88888

Dear Ms. Editor:

Please let me know if you can use the enclosed 1,000-word piece, *Porn Story Extraordinaire*, for Porn Magazine.

I look forward to hearing from you.

Sincerely,

Hopeful Author
12 Lover's Lane
Suburbia, TX 77777
P(555) 555-5555
F(555) 555-5555
pornauthor@whatever.com

Queries

A query is basically a proposal. You have a great idea for a piece and you want the editor to let you, and only you, write it. Queries are mostly, especially in this genre, used for non-fiction, although a fair number of porn magazines don't require them. Instead, they ask that you send complete manuscripts of both fiction and non-fiction. That's good for the beginning writer since a good query often includes a writer's credits, and if you don't have any it's best to just let your manuscript speak for itself.

For those that do require you to send a query, be just as professional as if you were submitting to a mainstream market. A great idea will get you nowhere if it's not presented appropriately. While editors that I know personally respond just fine to a one-line e-mail presenting my proposal, an editor that doesn't know me is likely to think me rude at best. And keep it simple, no more than a few paragraphs, and certainly no more than one single-spaced page. I like to double space between paragraphs on queries, it looks a little neater and less overwhelming.

Here's where you get to blow your own horn, albeit not too loudly. No editor likes a show-off. But you *can* tell him about the markets you've sold to and the articles you've written and why you're the perfect one for the job. No credits yet? That's ok, but don't invent any – and please don't say something lame about how you're not published yet *but if only* you were given a chance...blah, blah, blah. Better to just stay mum on the whole subject. Wow 'em with your subject and your superior writing skills, and you don't *need* credits.

What follows is a sample query for a celebrity interview, a more or less true piece that deals with a real (at least here in how-to land) porn star.

Sample Query

Start with your correctly spelled header sent to the appropriate editor. Then, hit him right away with a paragraph that will pique his interest.

Just what is it about Brittany Boobs that has set the nation's nightclubs on fire? Is it her generous nature and the fact that she volunteers twenty hours a week at the local children's shelter? Is it her out-spoken charm and the delicate beauty that won her the Miss Hometown Pageant USA three years running? Or could it be that little girl voice that manages to sound both innocent and sultry at the same time? Brittany herself doesn't claim to know the answer, but she scoffs at her do-gooder image. "Honey," she laughs, "I think it's just my tits they're interested in!"

Follow up with how you'd present the article.

I'd like to write an article for Big Boob Magazine on the amazing career of Brittany Boobs. From small-town girl to national porn queen, she's won the hearts of men everywhere. I propose a 3,000-word profile that follows her meteoric rise to the top. The main source for my article would be Brittany herself, but I would also include interviews with those who know her and love her: Her co-workers, family, and teachers at the children's shelter.

Then let the editor know why you're the one for the job.

As a freelance writer of erotica, I have sold over fifty fiction and non-fiction articles in the last two years. My magazine credits include Big Tops and Mountain Mamas. I am uniquely qualified for this particular story, however, because of my association with Brittany. You see, I am her mother.

Clinch it by wrapping every thing up neatly...

My writing is polished and precise but also accessible. Combine this with my knowledge of the subject and I think we'd have a winner of an article!'

Finish with a politeness or two...

Thanks for your time. I look forward to hearing from you.

And you've got a winning query.

Queries for the more fictitious articles can work more or less the same way. You'll want to focus on the slant, the word length, your credentials. You'll especially want to show off any knowledge you have about this particular market or subject so that the editor knows that you'll slant the article in the appropriate way.

To sum up query basics:

Use your first paragraph as a well-written intro to your piece – here is where you catch the editor's attention, as well as the readers'. In the second paragraph, let the editor know what you would write and how you'd go about it. Your third paragraph should be all about you and about why you're the one (above all others) for this piece. In closing, be polite but professional.

Staying Focused

Most of what you'll read about "how-to-write" always includes the advice to always write each day. In principal, I've found that to be pretty sound advice, although it can be easy to discount, especially if writing is not your full time occupation. In can be very difficult to carve out enough time for writing in a busy schedule that includes work and family. Personally, the choice of whether or not to write daily was made for me when I quit my day job to write full time. Now it wasn't a matter of making time for writing but a matter of desperately sending out manuscript after manuscript to keep food on the table. Good motivator, hunger.

But for most, the choice may not be so clear. Many writers I know struggle with wanting to write but being unable or unwilling to find the time. Some of the more successful ones I know end up writing in the wee hours of the morning, either before the kids wake up or after they've gone to bed. Not very appealing options, I'll admit, but there is some truth to the idea that if you don't use it, you lose it. Maybe not altogether, but it's sure easy to lose your momentum if you only get to your manuscript once a week.

I've found that the more time I spend screwing around, even if I'm doing important work like cleaning out my inbox or saving files, the harder it is for me to get motivated once I do begin the actual task of writing. Getting started after a lull usually means a long transition phase of alternately staring at the monitor, checking my e-mail, followed by false starts and stops, and ultimately getting up for more coffee. Often I have to force myself to just *start*. But then once I've been at it for awhile, the words come easily and I contentedly tap away at my keyboard for hours.

While writing should never be a chore, like *real* jobs often are, much can be said for simple motivation and stick-to-it-iveness. Face it, you're not going to sell unless you write. A lot. I got lucky when I started writing and managed to sell fifty percent of the manuscripts that I sent out. I figured at that rate I could make a decent little living working very few hours a week. Wrong.

That nice fifty-percent acceptance didn't include the months long waits for editors to finally get back to me on those acceptances. Nor did it include the twenty-five percent of manuscripts that were one-hundred-percent ignored. I quickly realized that if I wanted to make a living at this I had to put out quite a few more manuscripts than I'd initially thought. Those fifteen hour work weeks were just not going to cut it.

But even knowing that didn't always help. It was easy to get disillusioned and distracted. Still is! But the sad truth is that nobody's going to pay me for cleaning up my files. Now I try to save that work for when I truly am between assignments and need a little break. Until then on slow days I usually just try to plug away until the motivation strikes.

Ok, but still there are times when you are simply uninspired. Bored. Every sentence you write sounds stupid. That idea that seemed so promising yesterday looks pretty silly on paper. Yes, you can continue on, tapping out word after word, sentence after grueling sentence. And oftentimes that will even work, allowing your brain to get past whatever block it's got so you can get down to business. But sometimes, writing just for writing's sake is an exercise in futility. It's times like these that require a little deviation from standard operating procedure.

Maybe you can't write, but you can sure do something writing related. Go out and buy some magazines or books, and spend your time reading and analyzing them. Go through your neglected files and weed through all the out-dated writer's guidelines. Update your business files. Write "to-do" lists and catch up on which markets buy which stories with which slants. At the end of the day, you'll still feel like you got something done, your files will be organized and you might even find yourself anxious to hit the keyboard the next day.

And, if not, if, after you've given yourself a break, you still find yourself not motivated, you might want to consider the old tried and true 'fake it till you make it' idea. That is, it doesn't matter if you don't feel like writing, do it anyway. Don't let yourself get lazy about writing, if you do, your sales will end up just as sluggish.

Another trick I use during "stuck" times is just to switch projects. Ok, so I can't for the life of me figure out a plausible scenario for this particular story, and I've been trying for so long that I'm frustrated and just want to quit for the day. Instead, perhaps I could at least write the sex scene, get that part of it done. When I'm done with that easy assignment I'll probably be motivated to move onto another project, maybe that non-fiction piece my brain has been fixated on. Then when I reach a stopping place there, like some research I really don't feel like doing, I'll go back and see if I can't figure out an ending to the fiction story.

Use whatever tricks or strategies you need to keep you from getting stuck. I'm a great believer in never trying to force a story or an idea, that attitude most often doesn't work. But I do have to be careful not to give myself too many excuses to be doing something other than writing. From chores to kids to instant messaging to taking a walk, distractions are plenty, but writing has to be my main focus. There are many (often good) excuses for not writing, make sure you always remember that there are more (and often even better) excuses to actually get it done!

III
The Art of Writing Porn

Who, Me? Write?

Beginning writers are often overwhelmed with doubts: *How do I know if my writing is any good? Does my story flow smoothly beginning to end? How do I know if a sentence, a paragraph, a story actually works?* They struggle along with their story, stopping themselves at every comma, asking these questions and more. By the middle of the story, when they've stopped and started so many times that they've forgotten where they are, the frustration gets to be too much and they throw up their hands...*I can't write!*

I know that I struggled with these same self-doubts for years, always wondering what it was that *real* writers had that I didn't. I'd look at my supposedly finished product and shake my head, knowing that somehow I just wasn't getting it.

And I wasn't, not for lack of trying, but because I wasn't *allowing* myself to get it. I was getting so caught up in worrying about the end result that I wasn't letting go enough to get to the very process of writing. How was I supposed to even get the words out when I was constantly second guessing myself, critiquing the whole thing as I went?

Sure all the pieces need to fit, everything about your story has to be more or less perfect in order for your manuscript to sell. But the key for the beginning writer is that perfection doesn't have to happen just yet.

I've heard it called an internal editor, that little censor that sits on your shoulder and points out all your mistakes. And it's a fine thing, that critic, a necessary thing even, but not right now, not at the beginning. If you let him have his way now, you'll find your creative process stunted, your artistic flow dammed. For now you just have to trust yourself. Later, you'll go back and find those out-of-place paragraphs, those silly sentences, those misspelled words.

Even now, as I write the first draft of this chapter, I only have a rough idea of where I'm going. I know that I want to explain the writing and editing process and I know that it's difficult to silence your internal editor long enough to get the words out. But that's about it. I'll just keep typing away, coming up with paragraphs and pieces of ideas. For now, I'm not even too worried about the beginning, middle and end. I know that after I'm done coming up with the basics and putting them down on paper, I'll be able to figure it out. I'll be able to break down all these words into manageable little segments and piece them together, adding and chopping, until they come to some semblance of order. If I'm lucky I'll have gotten it more or less right from the very beginning, if not, it'll just take a little more finagling one way or another. In the end this chapter may be completely different than the half-baked idea I have in my head right now but I have faith that it'll work, nonetheless. For now I have to just sit here and write.

That is, after all, the beauty of the first draft. It's *supposed* to be rough, it's supposed to be more of an outline than a finished product. For beginning writers especially, the idea that a work will be even close to perfect the first time through is an illusion. Sure, I can put together stories now that are pretty close. But that's after an awful lot of practice. And there are still those that throw me.

I'll start on some new project, all excited about it's plot or it's characters. But somewhere along the way, usually on the first or second page, I'll find myself stumped, at a loss for words. It's not that I don't have my story figured out already, I do. I know where I want to take it and how it should proceed.

Then I'll realize that I'm trying to write a final draft instead of a first draft. I'm criticizing every sentence, trying to make it perfect, before I go on to the next one. I'm back-tracking at the end of every paragraph, checking for structure and form. And I'm getting frustrated with myself because, for all intents and purposes, this is not really very good writing. It's sloppy and rough and just plain bad.

But once I recognize this pattern, once I've figured out why I'm so stuck, it's easy enough to rectify. I just turn the critic off and start writing. Knowing that no matter how rotten my writing is right now, when I'm done I will be able to fix it.

In the end, and after many false starts, I've learned that being a writer begins with hard work; you have to write, and you have to write a lot. First a story needs to be written down in it's entirety at least once. Then it needs to be gone over again and again until it flows, until everything fits. No matter if that process takes two tries or twenty, it's still the work that has to be done.

But to be a writer, there has to be more. If the starting process is hard work, the end is about learning to trust yourself. You need to trust yourself to get the story out in the first place. Can you write? Of course you can, anyone can write. The real question is can you let yourself write, flaws and all?

And then, once you can do that, you have to trust that you'll be able to learn to tell what's flawed and what's not, and how to fix (edit) the problem areas. Is there something about that first sentence or paragraph or word choice that looks or feels wrong? Then it *is* wrong, even if you don't understand why yet. Here, after you've identified your problem, is where that internal editor that's been slowing you down gets his chance to shine. Here's where you can let him have his way, play with the words, rewrite them, fix them. And don't let him stop until it *feels* right.

Because if sounds wrong to you, it's going to sound wrong to your reader. My husband always catches me on this. *That sentence just doesn't seem right*, he'll say, pointing out a phrase I'd known was a little off but thought I could let slide. Or maybe it was a word that was just a little too harsh, or a paragraph that was out of place. I'd known something didn't feel right about it but had decided to live with it or maybe had just grown tired of trying to fix it.

In the end, a good manuscript is nothing more than creativity, hard work and very good editing, tying a bunch of loose ends together into one pretty bow.

And it's probably a little easier and a little harder than you think.

The Basic How-To

When you're first starting to write porn, it's probably best to have some idea of where you want to go with a story. Later you may be able to wing it but for now have a character or a plot or an idea ready. Sometimes a really descriptive first sentence can serve a good starting point. Or an especially creative character or locale. Once you have a basic feel for what your story is going to say, the very best thing to do is sit down at your computer with your story idea and write it all down. Start to finish. If possible, do that all in one sitting so you don't lose your momentum or the tone of the story.

Just write. It doesn't matter if you were shooting for 3,000 words and come up with 6,000 or 2,000. It doesn't matter if every sentence sounds the same or if your setting is awkward or if your characters lack depth. At least not yet. There's time enough for editing and fine-tuning later. All that matters is that you have a story, with a rough beginning, middle and end. For now, just write

It doesn't even matter if you write it in order. Got a great idea for a sex scene? Write it down. Chances are good that by the time you're done with that part, you may have another great idea for the beginning or ending. Sometimes I'll get stuck on the set up, maybe it's too wordy or I can't figure out how to gracefully move my characters from the beginning to the sex. So I'll work on whatever's easiest, sometimes even blocking out three or more parts to the story and piecing them together later.

Then you need to follow that time honored advice and set it aside. Take a walk, get some coffee, sleep on it. Whatever works for you. I find that I need anywhere from fifteen minutes to several days between first and final drafts. I need to distance myself from the rough copy so that I can come back and critique my manuscript with an unbiased eye. I have to switch gears; going from Writer Mode; that free flowing author whose ideas just pour out onto the page, to Editor Mode; that nitpicking perfectionist who goes around cleaning up after the sloppy and self indulgent artiste.

Don't expect to be able to transition instantly from either of these modes or you'll set yourself up for failure. For awhile just let yourself feel great about the creation of your masterpiece. That's a very satisfying feeling, reveling in the success of having actually done it, gotten it all down on paper. Enjoy it. Give yourself some time to come down before you move into the next phase. Because the next phase can sometimes hurt.

Now you've got your rough draft. You did all the right things, wrote it all down then set it aside, got on with your dinner, your life. You're ready to pick it up again. Only now the Writer's flush of success is gone, replaced by the Editor's critical eye. Ack! It's awful! What a ridiculous bunch of drivel. Look at the grammar, the sentence structure, those incredibly trite adjectives! Who ever said you could be a writer?

Ok, you've got that out of your system. That was the easy part. The part where, before you were a real writer, you used to stop, throw up your hands in frustration and toss (or file - for those of us who can't bear to part with our words) it away.

But now you're in for the hard part. The part where you sit down again with your decidedly un-masterpiece and this time you fix it. Because it *can* be fixed. Whatever it's flaws, it can be fixed. That was the amazing discovery that I made some time ago; almost nothing I've ever written is bad enough to be discarded completely, some things just need a little more work than others. Maybe it needs a total overhaul or maybe just a little tweaking here and there, but it *can* be done. You just have to be willing to do it. And it's honestly not that hard if you believe it can be done and if you take it a piece at a time.

Structure

Start with the story as a whole. Break it down into it's beginning, middle and end. Make sure that you have all three, if you can't define them you're probably missing something. Is there a clear set-up (beginning), one or two sex scenes (middle) and an ending? If not, block them out. At this point you don't have to worry too much about the details, the words themselves, you're just looking for the basic structure. You may find that you're top heavy on one aspect of the story, perhaps your set-up lasted 1,000 words. Or maybe you left something out, maybe there's no ending, or only one sex scene. For now, fix your basic structure - give yourself three separate pieces to work with.

Once you've broken your story down into more manageable segments, you can begin to fine tune just a little. Let's say you've got your basics, beginning middle and end. Take one and work on it, manipulating it until it's a complete and coherent piece.

Beginning – Is your set up plausible? Could it really happen, at least in the fantasy world of porn? Do your characters have a presence? Are they well defined, do they have personality? Did you fit in all the details necessary to get the story started, to move it along?

Middle – Does the sex flow easily from your set up? Do you have two separate sex scenes (if needed) and are they relatively plausible? Do all the pieces fit together? Do the characters move from gracefully from act to act or place to place, or are some parts awkward?

End – Did you bring all the elements of the beginning and end together? Did you leave any loose ends or unanswered questions? Does it all tie-in nicely?

In this rough stage, as you notice things out of place with your beginning, middle and end structure, fix them. You may have to add some space between your sex scenes or move the participants to another location so the sex is smoother. You may even have to rearrange. Often I'll find a paragraph that just doesn't fit and I'll need to move it to a different part of the story. Or sometimes I have to get rid of large pieces of the story because the whole thing is too long or because once I got to the end, some of the beginning had become unnecessary.

Only when you've got your basic structure blocked out, your beginning, middle and end all there and accounted for, should you begin to dig a little deeper.

Paragraphs

I like to look at a paragraph as almost a separate story in it's own right.

Beginning – A paragraph needs a clear beginning that usually ties in somehow to the preceding paragraph. If it doesn't do that naturally as an extension of the last one, you have to manufacture it. Beginning writers often let their paragraphs jump randomly from place to place, making it difficult for readers to follow. Try to transition smoothly from one to another before you move on.

Middle - The bulk of the paragraph (the middle) is where each sentence has to fit into the paragraph's structure as a whole. If this paragraph is about your heroine's physical attributes, you need to stick to that. You may have written the perfect sentence about her motivations but if it's in this particular paragraph, it's going to be out of place.

In reworking a first draft I often I find that my sentences and paragraphs are jumbled together in awkward ways. I may have all the right information and all the right descriptions, they just need to pieced together in a different way. By going through each paragraph individually I'm able to ferret out those pieces that belong to the story as a whole but not to this paragraph.

End - After your paragraph has completed it's course and finished up it's particular thought process, it needs to somehow flow into the next one. As it's creator, you need to make sure the ending is put together in such a way as to take your reader on a seamless journey into the next one. If you don't, if your transitions are awkward, you're going to slow (or even abort) your reader's journey.

Sentences

Once you've dissected your paragraphs and decided that every sentence belongs, you need to look at each sentence separately.

Pay attention to how you begin each one. Are you always starting with the same word or phrase? Not only is that awkward to read but it's boring as well. You'll need to mix up your phrasing. And watch out for the word *then* at the beginning of a sentence. If you find yourself overusing that word it may mean you're not transitioning your sentences and paragraphs very well.

Aside from the beginnings of sentences, watch out for repetitive words within the same paragraph. There's no reason to overuse certain words, there are almost always plenty more available where those came from. Sure, when you're dealing with porn, it can seem like your resources are limited. After all, how many words are there for a particular body part? But to keep it interesting you've got to learn to be creative about re-structuring your sentences to keep from overusing the most obvious ones.

Vary your sentence length. If you have five sentences in your paragraph, try to make some short and some long. Throw in a compound sentence for variety, or maybe just a creatively used comma. See if your paragraph flows. If not, fix it.

Chances are, you'll intuitively know where your sentences and/ or paragraphs are falling apart. On some level I'm always aware when something's wrong or just doesn't fit, even if I'm not always sure exactly how to fix it. Pay attention to your gut feelings about your sentences and paragraphs, if they don't feel quite right to you, they won't feel quite right to your audience.

Some other details to watch out for

Porn, at least for the markets we're dealing with, is usually written from the first person. This can take many forms, from a simple stream of thought, as though the author were actually talking to his audience, to a quite stylized first person essay. You, as narrator/ participant/storyteller need to draw your audience in and first person catches that immediacy quite well.

There are really spectacular third person porn stories out there, or maybe there are some varying-person stories just waiting to be written (maybe I'll even try one when I'm done writing this book) but for now, especially at the beginning, stick to first person perspective for mainstream porn.

Speaking of perspective, is yours staying the same the whole way through? If you started by telling the story as if it were happening right now, have you stuck to that? A lot of beginners tend to switch tenses in the same paragraph. Keep your *she was's* and *she is's* straight. You can certainly switch between past and present in your story, but make sure that you've got obvious breaks between the two or you'll confuse yourself as well as your audience.

Personally, I tend to stay away from dialogue when writing porn. For other venues it works great, adding nuance and detail and vitality to your writing. But in porn so much of it comes out sounding stilted. Your characters, after all, are there for one thing, and it's not talk. Erotica obviously lends itself more readily to dialogue but even then I would be very careful not to overdo it, especially within the sex scenes themselves. I've run across too many stories where the prodigious use of *Oh, Baby!* and *Do it harder!* should have been left on the proverbial cutting room floor.

There can be, however, some use for dialogue at the beginning and end of your stories. Conversation between two people can often set your scene quite nicely, usually with a minimum of words, and can also add another character for your main character can react to. I also often use dialogue (sparingly) at the end. Sometimes a small joke between characters or a bit of verbal sparring can be just the thing to tie up a story's loose ends.

Avoid the overuse of description. Just like in mainstream writing, description is used far too much by novices. While it can be quite tempting to describe porn characters in terms of their physical characteristics, it's best to find other ways to get your story across. For example, I make it a point never to use the age-old 36-24-36 style of describing a woman. Whatever her particular attributes, try to find some other way than straight description to let your reader know. Let your unique choice of words *show* your audience how beautiful this woman is, don't speak down to them by just listing the details.

The Final Draft

So you've looked at and fixed your basic structure, you've organized your paragraphs, you've fine-tuned your sentences plus you've double-checked your tenses and perspectives. Now you need to run through the entire story again, checking the flow.

Watch for parts that seem to trip you up, whether it's awkward sentencing or confusing paragraphs. Read it out loud to yourself or to someone else to see how it all fits together. If a sentence or word sounds strange when read out loud, chances are good that it will do the same on the page.

I like to go through the story in it's entirety several times. Often the part that's been run through several times (usually the beginning) sounds a lot more polished than the rest. At that point it's simply a matter of working through the not-so-polished parts until they're all just as shiny as the first one.

Proof Reading

It's easy to skip this last step. After all, haven't you read through your manuscript about a thousand times already? Don't you know it all by heart? Wouldn't you have already caught a misplaced comma or a misspelled word?

Absolutely not! Quite the contrary, looking at the big picture can quite often blind you to the small details. You'll be surprised at how much you've missed. Especially if you've changed a lot of things from your first draft, it's easy to overlook the obvious.

While checking through a story of mine in a print magazine I caught a huge mistake that both the editor and I had missed. I'd started out this particular story with one name for my character but somewhere along the line her personality had suggested another so I changed it. Unfortunately neither I, nor the editor, noticed that at the very end the first name had been left in, leaving the readers wondering, I'm sure, who this brand new character was and where she'd come from.

This is where you need to check everything, your spelling, your grammar, your punctuation. Better yet, have another person check it for you. My husband almost always proofreads my finished products before I send them out. He considers it a perk of my profession. And he quite often catches mistakes that I've made in what I consider to be an absolutely finished manuscript.

A proofreader is also good for showing you the places where the story doesn't flow. If your proofreader is confused about something, your audience/editor will be, too. My husband often points out places where I need to add another descriptive sentence or haven't fully explained something.

By looking at his feedback as a valuable part of the process of writing, I'm able to glean valuable information as to what a reader or an editor will think. If you can, find a person who can help you in this way, someone you trust, someone who is capable of being both kind and objective.

But It's All Been Done Before!

Read any amount of porn and you'll soon wonder *How on earth am I going to be able to come up with anything new?* After all, there are only so many ways to actually *do* it, no matter how well you might be able to *tell* it. You'll start to believe that everything has been covered already, and that there couldn't possibly be even one new angle to any aspect of human sexuality. Well, you'll be right, at least about the first part. It has all been done; done, said, printed, and then done again. The same story lines, the same plots, and mostly the same characters. Here's where all that reading can sometimes get in your way. It's easy to get discouraged sometimes and believe that you can't possibly come up with a new spin on such a well-covered topic. But you'd be wrong.

Here's where (once again) you need to put away your negativity and trust yourself. You *can* do it differently, uniquely, your way. You, being a one-of-a-kind creation yourself, can put your particular spin on a tried-and-true story line – and make it not just different, but better. Your take on sex, from the actual physical aspects of it to the intense emotional aspects of it, is always going to be different than mine, or any other of the thousands of porn writers out there submitting stories. No matter how hard we tried, you and I could probably not write the same story. Our histories, our beliefs, our experiences, all would conspire to lead us down some different path. Allow your personality and imagination free rein and you'll find that you never run out of new and different slants on the same old story.

Which is not to say that magazines always *want* radically new and different slants. Remember, a lot of these magazines thrive on a more formulated structure anyway. They like their stories to have two pages of plot, two sex scenes that each last for three to five pages, and a cute but short ending. They might not *want* exotic new locales or mind-bending scenarios or back breaking new positions. They might want the old standard, just done up a little differently than the *last* old standard.

In this kind of situation your job is to give them what they want, a formulized structure, but also to make your story come to life within that structure. As one editor suggested, *It can be rather like acting: pick a character and make them breathe for me, different voice, different beliefs, different backgrounds, different ways of looking at things.*

One way to bring your story to life? That's easy – let your characters do it for you.

Characterization

Characterization can make the difference between a completely boring piece with some sex thrown in and a stimulating story that leaves your reader caring about what he or she read. Of course, there are other more base ways to look at it, such as the fact that well-rounded characters will put money into your pocket more quickly and efficiently than boring ones. If you want your stories to sell they must stand out from all the rest. They need a strong point of view, and that almost always means strong characterization.

Sure, most people looking at a sex story in a magazine want to get turned on. But they also want to connect with the characters. They want to think that the narrator or main character could be their boss, their neighbor, the stranger at the bus stop. They like to fantasize that this sort of thing might actually happen to them. It's your job to give them characters that are believable enough to let them think it really could.

Your characters don't just define your story. They *are* your story. For example, consider that perennial favorite, the Boy meets Girl at the Laundromat story. By taking this one scenario and changing the characters, you can completely redefine this story and it's market.

For the "younger woman/older man" market, your male character could be a recently divorced businessman in a Laundromat for the first time. The sweet college coed he recruits to help him learn how to wash his clothes could be oh-so-knowledgeable about laundry but sorely lacking in sexual skills. He would, of course, be glad to thank her for her help by teaching her some of the finer points of love-making.

For a more hard-edged market your guy could be a biker on his way through town. Looking just to wash his clothes he could also find some quick and exciting sex with the tough talking biker chick who runs the place.

For the "older woman" market, your heroine might be a sexy 40 something woman who's a bit of an exhibitionist and likes to seduce the young male college coeds that come wandering in.

Or there's the woman with great legs who likes to torment her secret admirer, the peeping tom. Or the couple whose secret lust for each other overpowers their better judgment as far as caring about who might be watching.

In each of these scenarios the setting, that rather boring and over-used Laundromat, didn't change. But the characters sure did. And in each case, switching characters and personalities completely changed the angle of the story.

Quite a heavy burden for a character, eh? Don't make it hard on them or on yourself, let them get their job done. In order to do this, they're going to need a little substance. Give them plenty of depth and personality, get to know them, become them, and your stories will often write themselves.

For me, characters are almost always the starting point to my stories. If I can come up with an intriguing personality, maybe someone I've seen or heard about or just made up, often the story idea will form itself in my mind. And just as often, trying to start without a character can be an exercise in futility. Until I have a strong feeling for at least one of them, I find that there's not much to write about.

One of the most interesting things about characters is that they can come from the strangest places, or from the most confusing of emotions even. For example, my husband and I had a conversation about an old girlfriend of his who had flaming red hair, something that he'd found quite attractive. First I was just a little bit annoyed at the fact that he could still find flaming red hair attractive even though I don't happen to have it. Then of course I was a little more annoyed because I personally have always coveted flaming red hair and wasn't, in this lifetime anyway, ever going to achieve it. Fine, then. What to with my tiny little fit of jealousy? But of course, turn it into a story.

I let the idea percolate a while and, over time and with much thought, my character slowly appeared.

Originally I named her Penny, but that seemed a little coppery, nice but not quite flaming red. So I changed her name to Cherry, allowing me to give her a little more depth by saying that she was nicknamed Cherry because she loved that particular flavor of Kool-Aid. Later, the *smell* of Cherry Kool-Aid could even figure as a small but sensory part of the story. I made her rather plump (since I was targeting a fuller-figured market) and pale in a porcelain sort of way, and I added lots of freckles. I fashioned her a little on the young side and very sweet, but not too naïve. Kind of free spirited, of the easy to laugh and hug variety. I got to know Cherry, to like her.

In order to fully explore Cherry's beauty, I figured I needed to tell the story from a male point of view. That of course, changed my narrator's voice so I needed to now get into *his* head, too. I wanted a character that would enjoy Cherry's spontaneity and charm and, of course, the freckles that covered most of her body. I decided that I liked the idea of a narrator worshipping her just a little bit, falling in love/lust from afar, and then having his dreams realized. So I put myself into his brain and watched Cherry in my head for a day or two or three.

He was just as nice as she was, kind of in awe of Cherry but still a well-rounded and fairly responsible sort. He lived in an apartment complex who's occupants included his best buddy and, course, the flaming red-headed woman he was about to meet.

Only after I'd lived with Cherry and her admirer for a while, felt like I understood their motivations, did I feel ready to start on the plot.

Plotting

The words "porn" and "plot" have long been used as opposites, as though you can't have one without the other. This is an undeserved rap in my opinion, but not without some truth to it. Certainly there are a few magazines that want no plot at all, they're looking for just the sex, please. But most porn for sale these days has some semblance of a plot.

How plausible that plot, is, of course, up for debate. It's not necessary that your scenario could, in real life as we know it, actually happen. It's more about what your readerships *wants* to happen. Do two college students ever meet in that Laundromat and do it right there on the floor? Well, probably not, or at least not very often. But does a college age guy reading a magazine want to think it does? Absolutely. Do voluptuous older women really answer the door in the nude when the pizza guy comes? That one's probably even less likely than the Laundromat scenario. But the guy that delivers pizzas (or the women receiving them) would sure like to think that it happens. If your audience can visualize it, so can and should you.

Your market will, of course, define your plot. Somewhere between the no-plot sex magazines that are looking for raw sex and lots of it and the literary markets that are looking for mostly plot but on the extremely sensual side, falls the majority of the markets, those looking for some semblance of story.

As a porn writer, you'll discover that, thinly veiled or not, plot is still mostly used as a vehicle to get from one sex scene to another. But that doesn't mean it's not important. A completely implausible plot doesn't allow your readers to join in, so to speak, to imagine themselves in the same circumstances. Play with your plots the same way you play with your characters. Invite your reader along for the ride. Help him believe that something he wishes could happen, really could.

A lot of your plot ideas and set up can usually happen in your head while you're working on other projects. It's not as though you need to sit down at your keyboard and agonize over your scenario. I think about my plot the same way I do my characters, in my head first, living with the different scenarios and possibilities for awhile before actually committing them to the page.

Cherry's plot developed in much this way. Before I wrote anything down I'd already figured it out in my head.

First I had to give them a way to meet. An accidental knocking on her apartment door solved that problem. I added a third participant, our hero's best friend, solely so that Cherry and the narrator could develop a friendship, so that his desire for her could build over time. This friend was a faceless, nameless and voiceless character though, so he wouldn't interfere with the more important dynamics. For my first sex scene I devised an accidental witnessing of Cherry in some solo action (hence the apartment building to begin with, he needed to be able to walk by her bedroom window and see her). After that it was a relatively simple matter to move them from friendship to (surprise!) sex partners.

Another relative easy and painless plot development, mostly done in my head while I was actually doing other things.

Which is not to say that this particular setup always goes smoothly. As the narrator to a story I was writing for the "smoking" market, I became a voyeuristic, very much obsessed male. I sat down at the keyboard knowing most of what I was going to write, and how I was going to get myself there. I was doing fine, very much into my character, and my plot was just cruising right along.

But suddenly, a particular sentence popped into my head and wouldn't go away. Unfortunately it was a sentence that changed my narrator into a woman. Doggedly, I kept trying to continue with my narrator as a male, but eventually I had to give in to fate and rewrite the story with a female point of view. Of course that didn't happen to work for the market I was targeting, the editor had specifically asked for a male narrator. So much for that sale.

The story did eventually sell, albeit a year later and to a lesser-paying market. But to this day, because I allowed it to dictate itself to me, it's one of my favorites.

The moral? <u>Trust yourself</u>. You'll know when things are right. If a plot or a character doesn't feel quite right, change it. Give your character a new name, a new age, a new motivation. Take your plot off in a new direction. Maybe give it a new location. On the other hand don't beat yourself up thinking that you always need new and unique plots to keep your reader interested. Feel free to let yourself write the old standbys if that's where you're leaning. When your stories begin to flow from you with very little effort, you'll know that you're following the right path. Sometimes, writers block is *nothing more* than an unwillingness to let yourself and your creativity be. Once you're able to do that, the next phase, coming up with ideas, will be oh-so-much easier.

Ideas

Lots of beginning writers get stumped on the whole idea thing. And yes, it can seem rather daunting. Once again, how many ways are there, really, to do it? Especially when you've done a lot of reading, it can certainly seem like there must not be one more original idea out there. But ideas can and should be the least of our worries. Using both our own insights and our surroundings as starting points, all we have to do is tap into that great sensory underworld.

Here are some examples to get you started:

• *Pick a sense.* Smell, taste, touch, vision or hearing. Or pick the sixth sense, if you like. Now, imagine that sense and something that you like about it. Do you love the smell of fresh coffee? How about making an alternative coffee shop your setting? Add a rebellious and much pierced young woman. Is she sullen and cocky, does she like to bed unsuspecting older men? Or is she older herself, does she like to bed her unsuspecting younger co-workers? Does she sleep with men? Women? Both? At the same time? Who could be her lover(s)? And how?

Play with your senses. If you were a character, what could you hear or see, right now that would pique your interest? Could it be the sight of a sensational pair of legs as you're sipping wine at an outdoor café? Or how about the low moan of a woman in pleasure, right in the next room? Maybe it's the sudden ring of the doorbell, bringing some new adventure straight into your lap. Where can those images lead you?

• **Pick a topic**. Office romance. The possibilities here are literally endless. What kind of office? Lawyers? Management? How about a construction office or a hair salon? Are your characters equals; two top-notch lawyers who hate each other at first, then end up doing it on the conference table? Are they subordinates; the sexy construction office worker and her foreman boss who finally have a fling? Are they the same sex; the two female hairdressers who aren't gay but find themselves stimulated by each other's provocative dress? Or do the two middle management employees get caught doing it after hours in their office and find themselves in a middle management threesome with their sexy female boss?

• **Pick a market**. Large-breasted women. How many story lines can you think of? Skew the point of view just a little bit. Make the narrator a man who doesn't even like big breasts. Doesn't like them, that is, until he meets Mary; the big-busted, big-hearted waitress at the diner down the street. Or maybe Mary, sick of men who love her only for her cup size, responds to her female co-workers' advances, thus changing her orientation forever. Or maybe Mary loves her big breasts so much that she also loves showing them off to as many of her customers as possible, leading her into all kinds of exciting, diner-related sex acts.

• **Editors**. After you've worked with editors for a while, they can help you come up with ideas. After all, they know their market and their needs better than anyone. If you prove yourself as a writer who can produce, you'll often be the first one to hear of those needs. One editor I worked with always gave me very specific instructions. She'd not only give me the basics of what she wanted – two college-age girls go on a road trip over the summer and have wild sexual experiences – but she'd also give me the specifics, too; make the heroine the shy, not-so-aggressive one, but have her catch the other one in a sex act, and have her be just a little bit surprised. While I tend to like to craft my own stories and plots, her way worked, too. I found that it was a good learning experience to be forced to create a satisfying story within someone else's parameters.

• *Brainstorm.* Brainstorming a subject or market with someone else (who's not necessarily a writer) can often lead to twice as many ideas. I've found that if I come up with a subject and present it to my husband, he can often think up suggestions that never would have occurred to me. For fun, I'll throw out a subject that I'm interested in, and then we'll think of ten different plots and ten different markets to target. (You can go a long way with the subject as simple as "outdoor sex" when you target it to such diverse magazines as "older men/younger women" or "blue collar working men attracted to (but not doing) the gay lifestyle," or "leg and foot sex"). Having an alternative viewpoint can open up avenues of ideas that might surprise you.

• *Play the "what if" game.* Ok, so your friend lost her virginity in the backseat of a car. What if someone were watching? What if she were caught? What if she liked being watched? What if she were with a woman? See how many stories you can come up with, and you might be surprised. Say a couple buys a new video camera. What if he videotapes her and they watch it together? What if it's discovered by the neighbors and they watch it together? What if they start a business and sell the tapes to their friends? What if he secretly videotapes her having sex with her best friend, *his* best friend, the mailman?

The Real Secret Behind Good Ideas

But nothing ever happens to me! – you may lament. Well I can't speak for all porn writers, but there's a good chance that nothing much ever happens to them either. After all they're sitting at their desks writing about it all day, that doesn't exactly give them enough time to be out there *doing* it, now does it? But that's ok because, not only is wild and abandoned sex not happening to us, it's not happening much to the rest of society, either. That's why they hire us, to pretend it does.

What does happen to us, or should be if we're going to succeed, are *fantasies.* And it's tapping into those fantasies that will provide more ideas than we would be able to write about in a lifetime.

Here's where you get to have more fun than should be allowed. Here's where *free rein* is the catch phrase of the career. Here's where you get to mine the incredible resources of not only your own, but your friend's, neighbor's and stranger's cache of personal experience and fantasies.

Because it's not only the things that you've done that will help you now, it's everything that you've thought about doing, everything that you've ever even briefly considered. It's true, every single sexual experience you've ever had can be turned into a story or two (or even ten), from losing your virginity to the time you did it in the pool to last nights romp in the marital bed. But every single sexual experience you've ever *thought* about or imagined can turn into another twenty (or fifty). Not to mention those many sexual acts that your friends or significant others have experienced or thought about. Oh, and then there's what you can *imagine* about someone else's experience.

My point? Personal experience, a willingness to ask others and a vivid imagination are all your best friends. Embrace them.

You're a human being. You have fantasies. Now is the time to exploit them, the time to play. You can change roles, you can change genders, you can change lifestyles. Imagine what it would be like to be your neighbor, your boss, a rock star, a transvestite. Get into your characters. Explore them. Quite often they will lead you to a story.

Take one of my exhibitionist characters. I'm not much of a show-off myself, but that doesn't mean I can't pretend to be one, can't try it on for size. And that doesn't mean I can't add in another one of my fantasy figures, firemen, to spice things up.

So after the firehouse near my home was renovated to accommodate what I assumed were sleeping quarters, I wrote a story about how said exhibitionist used that private, enclosed space near where the firemen slept to her advantage. Would I ever do such a thing? Hell, no! But I sure had fun pretending I would.

And then there was the virginal young thing that happened to catch a fireman's eye at the annual firefighter's car wash. He spotted her, of course, from clear across the room. Long ago, as a semi-virginal young thing myself, I had designs on a fire-fighting captain. So it wasn't too much of a stretch to imagine how it would have felt to have him catch my eye and have my fantasies realized.

Often, after I've found a starting point, maybe an intriguing character or an unfamiliar market, I'll discover that there are more fantasies tucked inside of me than I even knew. And once I allow myself to play with them, let those new fantasies have their way, I find that even more ideas open up to me.

Using your own more-or-less real self as a character

Consider leg and feet magazines. Not that I used to think much about them other than to laugh at my own size-ten feet and think that I'd certainly never have a man fawning over them. But, after reading several stories about the fetish, I realized that it wasn't about size. It was more about worship. So I wrote about a character remarkably similar to myself, size-ten feet and all, who happened to be appalled when her new boyfriend suggested some foot play but was gently and erotically led over to the other side. After all, it wasn't exactly difficult to imagine how great it would feel to have someone massaging my legs and feet.

Once I placed my (own more or less real) self into the equation and got into it, I could finally see the allure of the leg sex market. Suddenly it was easier to go deeper into it, exploring the darker aspects, like the domination and humiliation factors. Not that I'm even remotely into those mind-sets. But when I write my stories I am. When I'm that obsessed man, drooling anonymously over the sexy but out-of-my-league legs of my dominating co-worker, I am most definitely into that particular fetish.

Another example - As an non-militant ex (and sometimes wishful wanna-still-be) smoker, I could more or less kind of understand the smoking fetish appeal, at least enough to give it a try. Sure enough, once I started writing I found that there are plenty of erotic ways to describe smoking, plenty of ways to make it sexy.

Fetishes aside, anything you enjoy can turn into a story. Hikes in the mountains with my husband, sans sex, led to a story about a sexual adventure between man and wife in the Rocky Mountains. Getting a video camera of my own led to all kinds of stories, from the woman who tapes herself for her husband to the two women who videotape each other, separately at first, then together.

Ah, and then there was my brief foray into phone sex operator. Brief (actually non-existent) because the pay is truly awful. But before I bailed I did listen in on a few calls. I'd never known exactly how those calls were structured, but once I did I was able to put together several stories specifically about phone sex, where the character narrated on the page what she would be saying (or what the client would be hearing).

In general, feel free to base your stories on your own life, just embellish them a little or a lot.

Use your friends, lovers and acquaintances.

Yes, use them and exploit them. Trust me, they'll love you for it. One friend of mine has had the dubious distinction of being the character in several of my stories, sometimes just as a name, once as both a name *and* a story. I took her real-life story of losing her virginity and fashioned it (including all the participant's real names) into a cute, if a bit over-the-edge, thousand-word letter. Another friend's only slightly sexual experiences in the workplace gave me some great ideas for stories set in offices that were considerably more sexually oriented.

Other friends, of the true "younger women/older man" variety (she's 22, he's 37) have been endless sources of information for stories and also in providing quotes for articles. They're also good for ideas. This particular couple seriously flirted for awhile with a threesome. At last check they hadn't gone through with it but using their details and personalities I've been able to come up with two different stories. Don't be afraid to solicit ideas and actual experiences from people, as most of them are more than happy to talk about it.

I like to use and abuse the names of everyone I know, from friends to virtual strangers, to come up with characters. Names can be so evocative in and of themselves that the characters they invoke will often come up with plots of their own. Favored friends of course get the good parts, one friend's versatile name has been used for everything from a saucy teenage slut to a lusty older woman. And the not so favored friends, well they get the...um...bad parts, the snooty teenage sluts and the bitchy older women.

Or sometimes I'll pluck a person or a character, whole, right off the shelf. Maybe it's someone I've known forever or maybe just someone I've just met or seen, even a television character or show biz personality. You can just set all these different people down in the same plots and watch 'em go. Imagine, for instance how differently some of your favorite sitcom characters might react to the Laundromat scene. Write them all a part and see what happens.

Combine bits and pieces of your fantasies, your friends' lives, and a little truth here and there, and you can come up with all kinds of ideas.

You don't need to have participated in a three-way to write about a man and his wife having a spontaneous session in the hot tub with her best friend. But maybe you have a hot tub and know how good the water feels. Or maybe your friend has a hot tub and tells you about the time her friend started having sex with her boyfriend in said hot tub. It doesn't matter that your friend was terribly offended and told them both to leave, it only matters that a seed is planted in your brain.

And, you don't even have to be a man to write about how it feels for a man to experience sex. Ask your boyfriend how it feels. Ask him to describe it in detail – try to get him to think of different words to explain it to you. Then, read a bunch of stories written from the male point of view and see how they do it. How do they convey, to you the reader, what is going on, what words do they use to help you understand?

Ask questions of everybody who'd be willing to talk to you. You
don't have to be gay to write about a man's first experience with
another man. It wouldn't hurt, though, to have a gay male friend
to bounce ideas and motivations off of. After that, it's a relatively
simple matter to be able to imagine it, feel it, get into it.

Remember, mainly this is fantasy work. Have I done the things
I write about? Ha! Well, ok, maybe a few. I might even be an expert
on one or two of them. But mostly I've just fantasized about doing
them. Or I've read about them or talked about them. Or done
research for an article and become intrigued enough to write a
few stories about it. Sure, there might be some things you need to
experience in order to write about them but right now I sure can't
think of what they are. Porn is all about imagination and sensation
and creativity. If you're a decent writer, you surely can *imagine* how
certain things feel.

One of my best articles was the one I wrote on the subject of
water sports. An editor I was working with asked for it as almost an
aside. *Oh by the way, I hear that a lot of people are doing this peeing thing,
so see what you can find out, ok?* Um, well, all right. Now, this particular
activity was not one of the many that I had ever fantasized about.
Nope, this one was not even on my top ten list of things to try. More
like at the top ten of my never-to-even-think-about category. But,
hey, I'm flexible. I prepared to toss off a titillating article about it.

I dove right in. I subscribed to a newsgroup, did all kinds of
research on the 'net, and even found a counselor who dealt with
this particular kind of fetish. I discovered that this activity wasn't
necessarily just about kinky people who liked domination and being
different. While it did include those elements, mostly it was about
being born that way, and not having any choice about the fact
that those acts were sexual turn-ons. And it was about shame and
derision, and feeling misunderstood. Along the way I discovered the

specifics of the sexual aspect of it – just what the actual sensations are that turn these people on.

Ok, so in the end, I still wasn't interested in participating in that particular activity. But I sure understood those that were into it. And, armed with all that info, I wrote what I hope was a relatively informative article about the subject, plus I got a few fiction stories out of my newfound information.

So, you see, in the end, it's about being open. Open to talking, to fantasizing, to taking risks.

Just be creative and allow yourself to work with no inhibitions. Censor yourself later, or not at all. This is fantasy work. It doesn't have to be all that factual – let it just be fun.

IV
Story Specifics

Letter Basics

Even if you start out writing letters for free, just to get the hang of it, you'll find that most of them have a structure. Sure you could just string together a bunch of wild sexual exploits but you're going to have a lot better chance of getting even the free ones published if you stick to a format.

That said, in order to find out what their format is, you'll have to do plenty of reading. Since word counts and styles vary so widely for different publications, you wont find a standard formula for how many words go where. A reader-written letter in one magazine might run 600 words whereas a staff-written one in another magazine could go as high as 1500 words. Obviously these two letters are going to be fairly different in their structure.

They will, however, have some things in common. They all have the bare bones of a plot, a beginning, an end, lots of sex, and usually a fair amount of 'character.' By character I mean a strong lead voice that manages to get across, in very few words, the direction and slant that the letter takes. It is after all written by an actual participant and as such, needs to have a personality.

Is the letter written by a cocky college student with a lot of attitude boasting about his latest conquest? Or did a demure virginal prep school sophomore, shocked at what she's just done or at how much she liked it, pen this particular letter? Maybe it was a hard and sexy 45-year-old barfly, proud of her ability to bed attractive younger men? The tone of the magazine usually determines your character's attitudes and lifestyles but there's always a fair amount of room for play within those boundaries so be sure and have fun with the creation of your characters.

Let them carry your letter along, but also be careful to keep them somewhat in check. Yes, your character is a participant but he also needs to be a fairly well written one. Sure you can use slang or dialect or phrases of speech particular to your character. But don't get carried away with poor grammar or bad dialogue or sloppy writing in general.

You'll also need to be quite professional about your approach when sending your letters out for consideration. Just because Joe Blow the reader doesn't proof read and writes his letter in pencil on unlined paper doesn't mean you can, not if you want to get published and/or sell. Even in this relatively limited market, professionalism counts.

Speaking of limitations, letters can be fairly restrictive because of their small size. Six hundred words is not a lot of room to get your 'story' across. But even so, letters do have some semblance of a plot. There needs to be some reason for the characters to be in this situation, after all. Of course, it's usually not much of a plot, it can be as simple as *Husband talks wife into going to an orgy and they have a great time*. It's basically just a way for your characters to get to their goal, which is, of course, sex. All you really need to do is set them up so they can do so.

Writing letters can be great practice for learning to fit the most important details into your plot. What does your reader want in this market? Usually it's fast, exciting, sometimes surprising sex. Usually it's *not* the color of her eyes or the way the light glints off of her coppery red hair. In letters you usually need to cut to the chase and leave the more unimportant details out. You can save your grandiose plots and scenarios for the larger story markets.

Give your letter a little bit of a set-up, so you can introduce your characters and setting. Depending on the length of the letter, your lead in can last anywhere from one paragraph to three or four. Skip anything that doesn't matter, but do try to fit in enough sensory detail to give your reader a sense of where and with whom she is.

In a letter you can pretty much just jump right into the sex without too much dilly-dallying; your characters are there, they're ready, just let 'em have at it. Some letters will have more than one sex scene, depending on the length, but you might want to just stick with one for now. Same with multiple partners and sex acts. Don't give your characters too much too do or the reader won't be able to spend enough time on each act.

When the sex is done, your letter is just about finished. Letters don't waste a lot of time with cute endings. Even with the longer ones, a paragraph is usually plenty, and sometimes just a sentence or two will do. And since you're supposedly dealing with just a regular guy, you don't want to go overboard, often a simple *Boy are we looking forward to our next vacation!* will suffice.

Anatomy of a
Three Thousand Word Story

Even though it may seem difficult at first, writing a three thousand word story to spec is fairly easy once you get the formula down. Everything has its place in a story of this size. You just have to learn where and how it all fits together. Eventually you'll learn how to guesstimate that fit fairly accurately, you'll intuitively know whether the set-up is too long or if that last sex scene needs to have a few hundred more words.

But at first it can be difficult figuring out what goes where, and why, and how. It certainly pays to learn, though. Once you get this one down and figure out what the structure is and how to work within it, you'll definitely have a marketable skill in the world of porn. Not only is this story probably the easiest size to write, it's also by far the most in-demand.

The three thousand-word story has something for everyone, a fair amount of plot, enough room for some character development and plenty of sex. It's the perfect size for editors as well as the perfect vehicle for you to learn how to concoct a decent story.

Let's break it down into its parts. We'll begin, of course, at ...

The Beginning

Every story starts with some sort of lead-in, where the characters are introduced and the plot is set up. Traditionally the beginning lasts for less than a thousand words (five hundred is better) because editors like to see the middle (the sex scenes) by at least the third page. This means that in just a few pages, you need to set the tone for the whole piece. There's not a lot of room for excess here but your intro still has to convey all the necessary information. This is where your reader (and your editor) learns the basics, the five W's of the porn world - Who, What, Where, Why, and When.

<u>Who?</u> – This will be, almost invariably, the most important aspect of your story. Given the relatively limited amount of space you're dealing with – we're not talking novel length here - your characters can go a long way in helping your define your piece. Just like in letters, I like my narrator (who is often also the main character but not always) to have a definite personality, it makes for a much stronger story when he/she is memorable in some way.

No matter what persona you choose, use it wisely. Use words that fit your character's personality. Is he well educated or street-wise? Young or old? White collar or blue collar? Watch your phrasing and dialects. Young ditzy women aren't going to be using really big words but businessmen might (in fantasy land, anyway). The forty-something female bartender can cuss up a storm but the refined business woman better not. The leg sex seeker might snivel and whine about getting his girl but the macho carpenter sure won't.

Keep your targeted reader in mind, also, you don't want to offend them or write over or under their heads. The story about the two liberal conservation activists who meet in the forest and do it on the path won't go over very well in a more right-leaning publication. (Unless maybe you make them sniveling tree-huggers who only get to watch while the *real* men and women go at it). For a blue-collar magazine you might not want to use much computer-ese whereas for an upscale businessman's market you're not going to see as much trash-talk.

Use your narrator, much can be said for letting her thought process impart tone and setting. The more info you manage to convey about your story through the narrator, the less you'll have to spell out as fact.

That said, keep your characters to a minimum, you just don't need a lot of them. Too many people just clutter up your story and become difficult to deal with. When you're only working with three thousand words you can't waste your space on unnecessary words or people.

While they need to have personalities, be careful not to make them too multi-faceted. They can be smart or ignorant, deep or shallow, but try to concentrate on just one of two parts of their personality. Maybe your narrator is a lawyer, make him feel and act and talk like a lawyer but use the details of his job or hobbies sparingly.

Why? – Ok, so maybe it seems a little silly asking, "*What's my character's motivation?*" when writing a story like this. We are talking about porn after all. But even so, even within porn's limited plot structure, there still usually has to be a reason. And your characters are almost always the ones to provide that reason.

Why are these two (or more) people going to have sex? Is it because they're best friends who've always been sexually curious about each other or because they're obsessed about some facet of the other? Even if the reason is just that they're two horny young college students who happen to be thrown together (at the Laundromat of course), give them a reason to be there, a reason for wanting sex with each other.

Where? – Somewhere in those first few pages, usually in the first few sentences, you're going to need to *place* your characters. Whether it's an exotic tropical island or a suburban bedroom, they have to be somewhere. And even if it's somewhere relatively boring you can add details that make it interesting. One voyeuristic character of mine liked to sit in her kitchen and watch her neighbor. To add some sensory detail and fit in with her kind of creepy, obsessed personality I made her kitchen chairs vinyl, the lighting dim and dreary and the window she peered out of dirty.

Try not to just tell the reader where your characters are. Don't list detail after boring detail about the Laundromat's décor. Less can often be better when it comes to location but you need to be sure to give your reader a place to imagine. The sun could be painful to your character's bloodshot eyes; or the smell of the coconut suntan oil could permeate the air; or the seagull's harsh cries could recede into the distance; or her kisses could taste like a cold strawberry margarita; or her skin could be baked by the sun and hot to the touch. Without using too many words you can help your reader *be* there.

When? This is similar to Where, in that it places your characters and your story. You can give it a specific time of day; a morning sex story might have a different feel than one placed in the late evening. Or you can give it a day of the week feel, a thank-god-it's-Friday story or a hump-day story. Or perhaps you can go for a seasonal feel, I personally really like summertime stories, they give me lots of sensory details to play with. But mid-winter blizzards and raging fires have their appeal, too.

Another twist, although not very commonly used in magazines, is to place your characters somewhere else in **time**, instead, say the Wild West or the fifteenth century. There's definitely a small market for this element in books, but it could also conceivably be used in a standard story also.

What? – Here's where you get to tell your reader what has already happened or what is about to happen. In porn stories, that's usually fairly self-evident. Your characters are more than likely going to engage in some sort of sexual activity. The only questions left are: 1. *What form is this sexual activity going to take? 2. Exactly what are they* *going to do?*

I like to "flavor" my stories early on. For a leg sex market I put in plenty of references, both subtle and blatant, to feet and toes and legs. A lot of this flavoring can be covered by your characters. For example, for a younger woman market, your character can narrate the story in an exaggeratedly innocent way, thus letting the readers know right up front that they're dealing with a virginal story line.

All right, you've got your five W's figured out, either on paper or in your head. Now you're ready for the next step, the Conflict.

Conflict

I know, it sounds like we're talking about a novel or a movie here, doesn't it? Along with *What's my motivation?*, now we need to deal with *Conflict?* Well, not all porn stories need a conflict, Boy can meet Girl at Laundromat and they can have sex and everything can be hunky-dory. But for a truly fun and memorable story, conflict has it's place. But don't worry. The kind of conflict inherent in porn is quite easy.

After all, you're dealing with sexual needs and desires. Meaning that conflict in a porn story is usually as simple as wanting what you can't (at least right this second) have. So, your character can be a virgin who desperately wants to have sex for the first time or a businessman who lusts after the boss or a obsessed exhibitionist who craves showing off.

Teasing and tension work great for conflict. You can begin to build on both or either themes early in the set-up and then continue them throughout the sex scenes. I use sexual tension a lot in my stories, from the woman who ties her husband up and won't give him an orgasm until the end to the simple tension inherent in the build-up to orgasm.

Don't forget the sex

And while we're still in the set-up phase of your story, here's one last piece of advice. Don't make the mistake of making your intro dry and boring and saving the sex for later. Your reader doesn't want mainstream fiction. Spice up your intro with words and phrases that suggest sex, giving the reader a taste of what's to come. You can make the whole thing really sexy right from the start or you can lead into it gradually but either way, your reader needs to know early on that these characters are definitely interested in sex.

And now, the part of the story we've all been waiting for...

The Middle

Yes, sports fans, this is where we start to get down and dirty. This is where we get to the *good stuff*. Of course, this can also be where you get to the disjointed part if you're not careful.

Transition #1

One of the reasons for keeping those intros fairly sexy is so you can segue gracefully into the sex scenes. If a good intro is kind of like foreplay - titillating, stimulating, and leaving your reader wanting more - the last thing he needs is a cold shower via an awkward transition.

No, if you're doing it right, he'll just move right along with you, from the more 'informative' part of the story into the more 'stimulating' part.

In much the same way as you find a way to tie your paragraphs together, so must you merge these two segments into a whole. Make sure that your intro, while it's giving your reader all the information he needs, is also slowly but surely leading him to this point. One of my favorite ways to do that is to have my narrator, talking in a conversational, stream of consciousness type of way, actually speak of the transition himself. Such as *Given all that, I'm sure you can understand why I had to do what I did next...*

If you find yourself getting stuck in this particular transition, read some short stories by other authors. There's no one set way that will work for each piece since each story's set-up will unfold in it's own unique way. But by reading plenty of stories you'll see how different authors handle different transitions and it will give you ideas for your own.

Sex Scene #1

The first sex scene of any story is *not* usually the hottest one. While it should of course have all the elements - a sex act or two and usually a climax - it's almost always the shorter and less intense of the two. Basically you want to save the best for last.

This doesn't, of course, mean that it should be any less graphic than the scene to follow. You don't want to spare any of the gory detail. This one needs to be very hot, just not as hot as the next one. If you've managed to keep your intro down to about 500 words, your first sex scene can run around 750 or even 1000 words Sometimes you can get away with no climax in this first scene but only if building that tension is part of the story.

I try not to use the same sex acts in each of the two scenes, it can get boring for the reader. Unless you manage to vary it some other way, say you choose a different locale for the second one, try to give your characters some variety in what they do and how they do it. I'll often use masturbation and/or fantasy for my first scene, that way my characters have plenty of other options to choose from for their big finale.

Sex scenes are usually just plain fun to write. As you write more of them, rather than having them get more boring, you'll probably find your own style and be able to experiment even more. Hopefully you'll get carried right along in the excitement of your story. Give yourself plenty of room to find your own voice, you'll probably be surprised at what comes out. Holding that internal censor at bay is even more important at this point of the story, now is the time for you to really let go. This is where you get to explore your own fantasies and dreams as well as play around with helping others to recognize theirs.

Just as in the rest of your story, don't just describe, let your reader feel what's happening along with you. Help him get so caught up in the scene that he forgets he's not actually in it. Use those senses again. Let your reader in on the sounds, tastes, smells and other sensations that are going on. Now's a good time to experiment with words, to really work at expanding your sexy vocabulary.

Hands moving down a body, for example, can alternately *slither*, *slide* and *slip*. Or they can *snake*, *lazily trace* or *massage*. Or, for a different feel altogether, they can *manipulate* or *squeeze* or *pinch*. Really feel what's happening to your characters and then explain those feelings to your reader in minute detail.

The first scene usually (but not always) ends in a climax for one or all of the participants. Again, this is not the time for the biggest and best fireworks. Save your truly big display for later in the story.

Transition #2

The end of the first sex scene can often be another difficult transition for the writer. You've got to gracefully extricate your characters from the situation they're in and place them in another one. One way to do that is to just continue the sex scene as is. But even the best scene can get boring if it goes on endlessly. Your reader really needs a change of pace. About 100-250 words is the norm.

If you're using the same characters and don't want to change the setting, your characters can always just take a break. Napping, talking, eating, all have been used effectively to give a breather between sex scenes. Or the partners can change, your main character can move on to her next conquest. Another option is that your characters can meet again but on a different day or perhaps in another location.

Sex Scene #2

This second scene is where your characters finally get to strut their stuff. What that doesn't necessarily mean is that they should show off how many different sexual acts that they could fit into the space of 1000-1500 words. While some porn writers can pull this off, it can be difficult to try to describe several different sex acts and have them all get the attention that they deserve. For now you probably need to stick to just a few. Let them have their sixty-nine and regular intercourse but skip the other too-numerous-to-mention possibilities for now. I find that I actually prefer this method, that of writing scenes that are more narrowly focused. I can often spend the entire scene on just one actual act, describing each part of it in intimate detail

This doesn't mean that you skimp on graphic description, of course, just because you're limiting the actual number of acts. Here's where you want your descriptions to shine. This is the moment your reader has been waiting for. Don't disappoint her now!

Use all that sensory talk that you've been thinking and reading about. Really explore the details of your scenes, from where your characters are to what they're wearing to how they feel. Here's where you get to pull out all the stops. Be your most graphic and your most detail oriented.

I've been amazed at how much I really have to say once I get started. As a matter of fact, three thousand words isn't nearly enough for me to feel like I can truly explore my characters and their sexuality. If you can let go enough to fully appreciate your characters and their physical as well as emotional feelings, you, too, should be able to find an excess of words to describe it to your reader.

For your grand finale, make sure that your climax scene is at least one full paragraph. While this part can seem rather tedious (even I can't find too many more ways to describe yet another orgasm) it's critical to your story. At this point you don't want to let down your reader by using only one or two boring sentences to describe this moment that he's spent the entire story waiting for.

The Ending

Porn stories don't usually just drop out after the last exciting sex act. Just like any good story, there needs to be some kind of closure. Often that closure is a bit of humor or dialogue or sometimes a realization that perhaps this should have happened a long time ago. When I get stuck on an ending I usually go back through the story. Perhaps I find the central conflict and resolve it with a joke. Or maybe I use a particular theme and expound on it. If I can't think of a good ending, it's often because of some mistake I made earlier, say, not giving my characters enough conflict or failing to describe a personality trait well enough for it to carry through to the end. Sometimes I'll need to go back and rework part of the story so that it flows gracefully into closure.

I've found that endings don't have to be long. Expounding endlessly on some facet of your story at this point can be boring. One well thought out paragraph will do, sometimes even a sentence can work if it ties your story elements up neatly.

Naming Your Story

More often than not your story will name itself while you're writing it. A central theme will emerge, or maybe it's a phrase or a character. I've used the names of some of my more engaging characters for several of my stories. *Rita*, for example, is about a 40-something seductress and a younger man who's lusted after her for years, *Pleasing Sylvia* concerns a blonde Goddess-type and her worshiper. A popular phrase can often work, like *Talk To Me, Baby*, a story about phone sex, or *Community Service,* about the young woman who met her intended at a fund-raising car wash.

If you're having trouble finding a suitable name, check to make sure that you've got a clearly defined theme in your story that *can* be named. There have been times when I've had to go back and add more detail to a story because it's overall concept wasn't clear.

Don't send a story submission out until you feel like you've got the perfect name. Better to wait a day or two for inspiration to strike than to give the editor the impression you don't know your own material well enough to name it. And, while a great name alone never sold a story, a catchy title doesn't hurt when it comes to editor recognition.

The Non-Fiction Article

Ok, so some of the non-fiction articles in men's magazines are true. As a matter of fact, in the big mass marketed mainstream magazines they're all true. The interviews are real, the releases are signed and the credentials of the writers are impeccable. Obviously those celebrity interviews and investigative news pieces are about as accurate as their editors can make them. And once you've got some work in the less mainstream porn magazines you could even try your hand at them.

But until then you can always have a go at the *other* non-fiction, that extremely fun, if somewhat falsified, non-fiction article. You might say that this particular flavor of article is it's own type of fiction in disguise.

These articles can range from the blatant, out and out, *Every single word is a lie*, to the more subtle, *Most of it's true except for the quotes*. Of course, even some of the articles that are mostly made up can have plenty of truth in them.

I've done a lot of research for some of the articles I've written, especially those having to do with health issues. My article on water sports included hours on the Internet, reading stories and articles, perusing web sites and talking to participants. In the end some of the quotes were made up and some real (plus there was another liberal dose of 'reality' added by the editor) but the gist of the article was true.

I've done the same thing with other non-fiction pieces, say for articles about anal sex and losing weight and eating healthy. Filled with good, solid advice, the basics in these articles would have held up in any publication. It's just the details that were made up.

And then I've done some completely made up articles, instructive little pieces all, with decent information and again, good solid advice, they just didn't happen to be true.

No matter, the premise is still the same.

Most articles in porn magazines deal with the how-to or the helpful advice. How to get laid, how to meet women, what older women want, what younger women want. What to say or not to say, how to act or not act. Or they concern something that either the reader or his girlfriend is interested in, fast food, say, or Japanese anime. At first I couldn't figure out how these writers and editors got their ideas. I mean, once you've done one article on how to meet women, haven't you done them all?

Well, not really. With articles, success comes with narrowing your focus. Sure one article for the "younger women/older man" market can be *What Young Women Really Want (and how to give it to her so as to get lucky yourself)*. But there are plenty of subcategories within that framework. What does she want sexually from an older man? What is she interested in when dating an older man? Is she looking for security or money or love or sex? Pick one of these topics and expound on it, keeping your focus narrow.

The non-fiction article isn't nearly as tightly defined as the average three-thousand-word fiction piece. There's no strict formula that they all follow; each magazine, as well as each format within the magazine, is going to be slightly different. Thorough reading of your targeted markets articles will, however, give you a pretty good idea of what this magazine is looking for.

Analyze these pieces just as you do the fiction stories. You'll want to pay attention to tone and style. Your slant makes all the difference. Here's where that character development you've been working on can come in handy. That article on *What Young Women Really Want* could be quite different depending on who it's "author" is. Is it a young college coed, all giggly and coquettish, or is it a seasoned older man, giving sage advice? Conversely it could be harder edged young woman - a bad girl - telling it like it is, or a less experienced man bemoaning the lack of advice out there for men.

Look at the magazine's usual formats as well as the actual editorial content. Do they use a lot of surveys or quotes? Are the articles mostly how-to, and if so what topics come up regularly? Combine what you find with the information from the writer's guidelines and you'll probably get a pretty good feel for this market's needs.

My first fumbling attempts at non-fiction came by accident, via an editor who needed content. I'd sold several fiction stories to her and she asked if I'd ever tried my hand at non-fiction. I hadn't but that didn't faze her, she thought I should give it a try. It turned out, after much direction and some serious hair pulling on my part, that I actually could write non-fiction. Although now, looking back, I have to say that at that point I couldn't write it very well. Luckily, my editor was satisfied enough and I had my first non-fiction sale.

That's not to say that it was all so easy, though. I struggled through the next couple of assignments before I really got the hang of it. Just like learning how to write fiction and structure a story, this new process was difficult for me. But after a bit of practice I began to really enjoy that process and now I have more ideas for articles than I know what to do with.

When it comes to selling your non-fiction, keep in mind that editors like to work with writers they already trust. It can be hard to break in with a query at some of these places. If you find a magazine that will accept non-fiction manuscripts without queries first, go for it. Go ahead and write one on spec and gear it specifically toward your market, just like you do with fiction. Or, if you've already sold a few fiction pieces to a particular editor, work up a professional sounding query with a good solid idea. If an editor's seen (and bought) your fiction, she'll be more likely to hire you for some non-fiction.

And of course it goes without saying that once you have an assignment, you stay true to your word and *always* produce what and when you say you will.

The Basic Format

Even though non-fiction pieces can vary greatly, and their word length can run anywhere from 500 words to 5000, they still have the basic *Beginning (Intro), Middle (Body)* and *End (Outro)* format. Once you've figured out your topic you can break it down into these more manageable pieces.

The Intro

You'll want the first intro sentence to be catchy enough so that your intended reader/editor will be intrigued and want to continue. Draw your audience in with something outrageous or titillating. This sentence also usually sets the tone and the content for the intro itself, in that it tells the reader what he's about to read.

The rest of your intro should concentrate on letting the reader know what's coming. Introduce him to the subject, tell him how you're going to present it and with what slant. The intro is basically the informative promise of what's to come.

Given non-fiction's varying word length, there's no real standard for how long an intro can be. But for my own articles, which usually run between 2000 and 3000 words, I try to keep it to just three or four paragraphs. Any more and you can bore the reader, plus the more intro you have, the less room for the body of the article.

The Body

This is the meat and potatoes of your article, where most of your quotes and information will go. There are two standard ways to present it.

Subheadings and bullets are common and easy. Your article doesn't necessarily have to flow easily from point to point. It can be broken up into more manageable segments. For example, in the *Where To Meet Women Article*, there could be subheadings for all the different places.

A little more difficult is the straight article, which is all text. This is a little more like a fiction piece, here all your sentences and paragraphs and ideas have to move gracefully from one to the other. It's a little easier to get lost in this kind of format, easier to lose your focus. If you attempt this one make sure your final editing process is thorough, to catch any inconsistencies or awkward spots.

Your editor may be the one to decide what kind of format you'll follow and how long each section should be. One editor I worked with had a very strict formula for her articles. She wanted an intro of three paragraphs and each paragraph after that was to have two quotes, the first relatively short and within the first sentence or two, the second a little longer and obviously toward the end of the paragraph. Sometimes direction like this can make your life easier, helping you to structure your story. But it can also occasionally get in your way, sometimes it's best to have a little more freedom as to where to strategically place your quotes.

The Outro

I've seen plenty of non-fiction articles that just plain end, there's no outro, just the presentation of the last point. Personally I think readers prefer some kind of ending. Just like in fiction, it's best if there's a nice, neat closure. Unlike the intro, though, outros don't have to be very long. After all, you've presented most or all of your material already. Usually a paragraph or two will do.

Here's where you tie things up, perhaps repeating some points that you made at the beginning, then leaving your reader with something catchy again.

If you're having problems getting closure on your article it may be because you haven't presented your points as clearly as needed, or perhaps your focus was a little disjointed. Check to make sure that your article stayed on task, that it didn't meander in too many hard to follow directions

After you've got all your article pieces put together, check to make sure that your outro matches your intro. Did you really do what you said you'd do in the intro, did you give them the information you promised? If, for example your intro said that you'd teach the reader how best to approach women in bars, did you follow through? Did you stick to that or did you maybe veer off into something unrelated and never quite get back on track?

Sidebars

After you've gotten through your first few articles and are feeling comfortable with them, you might want to try your hand at sidebars, those little information filled boxes within an article. Usually containing information relating to the article, like interesting statistics or sources for more information, they can make your piece look more professional. Some magazines will pay more for this information, some not, but even if there's no extra pay, the experience of putting them together will be good for you.

For a how-to article on anal sex, my sidebar basically listed my sources as places the reader could go for more information. I'd researched a few print books and also had found some interesting sites and articles on the 'net. Had I or my editor wanted more, my sidebar could also have listed places to buy toys, perhaps, or groups catering to that predilection, or maybe it could have referenced interesting statistics on the act itself or quotes from participants.

V
Working With Editors

Editors. Some days, it feels like a classic no-win situation: you can't live with 'em, but you sure as hell can't live without 'em. And you can count on the fact that there are some days when they're feeling the same way about us and our ilk.

Regardless of the frustrations on both sides, though, what is clear is that we need each other. They need us to create fascinating and titillating copy to fill up the empty slots in their magazines and we need them so that we can actually afford to stay home to write and still manage to buy groceries. But without mutual respect and communication, neither side is going to get what we want.

Some Basics

Don't ever assume it's enough to just send out your manuscripts. That's only the beginning. If you're lucky enough to receive any personal communication from an editor be sure and follow through on it as soon as possible (without overdoing it). Reply simply and politely to any e-mail that you receive, but only once. Return phone calls as soon as possible. Editors are always working on a deadline. Whatever information they need from you they actually needed yesterday, so don't delay.

Above all, and no matter how much you may want a particular assignment, never promise anything you can't deliver. The editor that's sitting there the day of the deadline with 3,000 words worth of empty space to fill because you didn't come through is most definitely going to remember your name, you can count on it. If you feel that there's any chance at all that you might not be able to get the job done, don't take the job in the first place. Better to lose the story right up front than incur their wrath this way.

Of course, it goes without saying to always present your most professional self to an editor. Sure, they know that you're a person with a life but he probably doesn't care. Don't bore him with personal details and don't assume a friendship that is probably not there. Remember that this is a business relationship and act accordingly.

There's also the politeness factor. Both writers and editors tend to forget this one. Common courtesy goes a long way. It's wise to never show an editor that you're annoyed at him or her, even if given ample reason to be royally ticked off. You don't have to necessarily like the game that you may be forced to play with a particular editor, but either play it with a smile or move on. And while you're at it, try not to burn your bridges. Editors may turnover quickly but they also have long memories. Don't blow your chances by being anything less than the consummate professional, always.

One of my favorite rules-of-thumb: Once you've got a market acknowledging your existence, keep it up. On the day they send back a rejection or an acceptance, have another manuscript ready to send out to them. Keep your name and your words fresh in their memory. Porn editors are very busy people and they don't have a lot of time in each day to think about your stories. But if you're polite and persistent – and on target – they will eventually take notice of you. Once they do contact you with an acceptance or an assignment, it's your job to make life easier for them.

I still remember the first time an editor e-mailed me. It concerned a short story I'd sent out for her consideration. She'd already bought a few of my stories and was interested in the one she had on her desk. She had plenty of fiction pieces that were similar to my story, what she needed was a completely different slant. Could I revise the story to fit her needs?

I could and I did, even though I was relatively unfamiliar with that particular slant. But she gave me plenty of direction and support, and we ended up with a fairly long-running relationship. I was able to contribute regular fiction to her magazine, instead of just the usual occasional story, for over a year. And as my name became better known by the other editors at the publishing group she worked for, I was also able to write for some of them as well as do some emergency write-ups for their Web page, dealing via e-mail with the editor-in-chief.

It's not only positive contact from an editor that you need to take note of, however, negative feedback can also help you in your career. While you may be tempted to ignore it, viewing all rejections as a bad thing, try to listen to editors who tell you why they weren't interested in your manuscript. Editor feedback is an invaluable tool. No, you don't have to like what they say or enjoy the way they present it. But there is often a grain of truth in even the most abrasive editor's remarks. If you can try not to take it personally, you can learn from their comments.

I didn't much like it when an editor told me that perhaps I should reconsider whether a particular topic was the "right one for me." Seems that since my lead character was fairly negative, she assumed that it was *me* talking, not my character. I wasn't terribly pleased with her assessment, but when I reread the piece, I realized that she was right. Not about the topic or my suitability in writing about it, but yes, the character was awfully negative.

In another market that piece might have worked, but not in this one. I re-wrote it according to her specs, exorcising any and all negativity – and she promptly bought it. In the end, I'm still not overly fond of this particular editor's style. But by now, I sure know her market. And I can almost always sell to her, as long as I'm willing to put up with her sometimes off-the-mark assessments.

One of the more frustrating aspects of dealing with markets and editors is that, try as you might to be professional, not everyone returns the favor. You may conscientiously and consistently follow through on every aspect of communication and find there are still plenty of markets out there that will never acknowledge your existence. While it's true that you deserve a response, whether you're writing to obtain writers' guidelines or sending in an unsolicited manuscript, you don't always get one.

I can't even count the number of times I've sent off for guidelines and never heard back. And then of course there are the countless manuscripts that have been sent off into no-man's land, never to be seen again. Queries and letters and phone calls go unanswered until I finally am forced to give up. Don't let a few of the bad ones discourage you, though. There are plenty of polite and professional editors out there who are actually interested in what you have to say, and who will respond appropriately.

Yes, it's hard to continue to send material out into that great void. Does anybody really know you're there? If a writer creates a great story and it sits, unnoticed, on a slush pile until it finally ends up in the trash can, does the story then suck? It can sure feel that way. But there's only one way around that. **Send your stuff out**, religiously and regularly. Eventually, after you've been rejected many times, some editor, somewhere, will contact you and you'll be on your way.

Once you have a relationship with an editor you have his or her ear, and it's obviously easier to sell again. But, remember that you're dealing with only one editor with a limited amount of space to fill (not to mention the fact that when he or she moves on, you'll have to forge a relationship with the replacement), so you need lots of editors on your side. ***Keep sending your material out.***

VI
Never, Ever Give Up

So, the first fifteen of your short stories have been rejected. Or, worse yet, ignored. You're frustrated and confused and thinking that maybe you should consider a career in Animal Husbandry or Hotel Management, *anything* besides writing. But you're not sure, should you really give up? Are your stories not selling because you're a lousy writer? Or is it because you haven't targeted your market correctly? Or is it just *because?*

There are so many reasons for rejection

Maybe it's because you're not following the writers' guidelines exactly, or it's that the guidelines themselves are outdated and the publishers are no longer even accepting what you're trying to sell. Maybe the editor you're writing to is no longer there. Or perhaps the quality of your writing hasn't progressed yet to the high-end markets and you need to concentrate on the lower-paying markets for a while to build your skill level up. Or is it only that a particular magazine is full of fiction right now? Who knows, it could be that the editor doesn't like your name, or maybe he's just out of town and your story is still sitting on a desk somewhere.

Maybe it's all of the above or maybe one of those reasons fits each one of the rejections you've received. Unfortunately you don't know which impersonal rejection merits which perhaps justified reason. The truly frustrating truth is that often there is no way to tell why certain stories are being rejected.

Sometimes, as you get to know editors, they'll give you feedback and suddenly it will all become clear. Of course they didn't buy that story, it was way too explicit for that particular market. Or vice versa, this market likes their talk sluttier and their sex hotter. Or maybe it's that the sex didn't start till page five and this editor likes it sooner, on page one if possible. Or, as you read more (or newer) issues of your targeted publications, you'll realize that you've been sending out stories that are slanted in just *slightly* the wrong way. Not to mention the obvious, that as you continue to write, edit and proofread your stories you can't help but improve. Maybe your early stories just weren't plain good enough.

But in the beginning it's hard to tell. And it's very easy to give up.

Don't.

It's as simple as that. ***Don't give up.***

Real writers don't give up. Real writers struggle along, honing their craft, figuring out their mistakes and learning from them until, finally, it pays off. Real writers look back on their early work and say, "*Good Lord, I actually sent this out?*" And then they fix the awkward sentences and the silly dialogue and they send it out again. Or they dust off another year-old manuscript and say *Hey, this one's not too bad, but I better fix this part before I send it out again.*

Real writers have learned a simple truth. Simply by writing every day - and not just rough drafts but polished final drafts, too - they've found that they've improved. And with that rise in skill level has also come a more increased awareness of their work as a whole and how others see it. Armed with that knowledge, they can look at their manuscripts and their markets with a fresh, less biased slant. And they, like you, can sell.

So, in the interest of practicing what I preach, here, to warm your soul and give you hope, is a personal example of persistence paying off...

The very first story that I sent out to a major men's magazine disappeared completely into the void. Oh, I did all the right things. It was a decently written little piece, professionally submitted. After hearing nothing after about four months, I queried and resubmitted the manuscript again. (In the meantime the two other stories I'd sent out had already been accepted so I did at least have the benefit of knowing that I *could* sell). Another several months of hearing nothing I politely queried again along with a notice that I'd pull it from consideration if I didn't hear from them.

Which, of course, I didn't. Being a little bit frustrated, and an uppity new writer and all, I wrote a letter of complaint about this magazine to Writer's Market, who in their turn, ignored me also. By now it was slowly beginning to dawn on me that perhaps not everybody in this business was going to play by the same professional rules that I was sticking to. But, undaunted and a just a tad stubborn, I sent in to the magazine for more writers' guidelines, thinking that perhaps I'd made a mistake or that something in them had changed. They were, word for word, exactly the same, except for this sentence in bold print at the bottom; **If we are interested in your manuscript, we will contact you.**

I wondered if this little addition had something to do with my persistence. Sure seemed like it. But I stuck to my guns, even though I figured that it was entirely possible that the editor in charge of receiving submissions knew my name and was quite probably burning all of my correspondence on sight. I didn't care. I was determined to break into this particular market.

As though nothing were wrong, I continued to politely send stories in for consideration. And I continued to just as politely withdraw them from consideration after 4-6 months. Until finally, one glorious day, I received a phone call from one of the editors – *not* the one I'd been submitting to. *We'd like to buy your story*, he said; and I tried to control my excitement. But as he talked I realized that he wasn't talking about the latest one I'd sent in. No, this was one I'd sent in eight months ago. One that I'd withdrawn from consideration about 3 months ago and subsequently sold (within two weeks, I might add) to their competition.

Sigh.

But yes, I'd be glad to send in others, which I did. Which he (surprise!) ignored. Except for one in particular that he rejected in a polite and nicely personal letter. I continued on, sending out manuscripts every four months or so, never sure whether anybody actually received them or not. Wondering (not for the first time) how on earth these people even managed to run a business.

In the meantime, I researched the market a little more. I read and reread the stories that this magazine published and tried to zero in on the market. I found more of a formula than I'd noticed before. Most of the stories were very similar. So I wrote one that was very specifically tailored to that market, one that I just *knew* that they would like, it was exactly what they used on a regular basis. And lo, they did like it! I was rewarded with a phone call just two months later from yet a different editor, (surprise! The one I'd been communicating with was no longer there), accepting the story.

I was asked to send anything else I might have along with the disk for the first story. So, thrilled that I finally seemed to have an editorial ear, I rewrote an old one and tailored it more to this magazine's specs, and also quickly wrote a new one, also geared exactly to their market. It wasn't till they'd both sold that I realized that the rewrite was the original first story that I'd sent out to them more than two years before!

Ah, and as if that weren't enough, there's still more...

About a month later, the editor called again, this time confused. The previous editor, the one I'd dealt with twice, once on an acceptance and once on a rejection, had set up a story for the next issue and had indicated that it was mine. But she had no contract. Was the story indeed mine? Doubtful, we went over the plot and some of the dialogue. Sure enough, it was mine. Of course it just happened to be the story that her predecessor had so politely rejected, in writing!

The moral of this story is obvious. You may never fully understand why you're being ignored or rejected or even accepted. Sure, if you're an intelligent writer, you might have clues, and they might even be correct. And the more experienced you get in this genre the more obvious some of your own (or your markets') mistakes may become. More than likely, however, you'll muddle about like the rest of us, just hoping for a big break. But that's okay. Muddling is all right as long as you learn from your mistakes and keep improving your skills.

And as long as you continue to be polite but persistent, and promise yourself that you'll never give up, you *will* see results.

VII
Now, Go For It!

Ok, you've read (and hopefully *re*read) this book and you've read and researched your magazines. You've sent away for your guidelines, maybe had a few amateur letters accepted and now your computer is purring gently in front of you, ready and waiting for you to begin. Now it's time to actually sit down and write.

So here comes the hard part, right? Here's where you're forced to slave over a hot terminal, tearing your hair out like all the real writers they show in movies, tossing crumpled up sheets of (virtual) paper into the trash can, right?

Quite the contrary, now it's time for you to have some real fun! Whatever else you get from this book, whether you choose to write professional porn stories or just craft well-rounded pieces for you and your husband to read and play around with, remember that this is what porn writing is all about: *Fun*.

Sure, it's also about fantasy and letting your imagination run wild and giving yourself the freedom to enjoy yourself. And, if you're good, it'll be about making a living. But for now, give yourself a break. Don't censor your first drafts, don't agonize over your mistakes. For now, simply write, allow yourself the freedom to be *just* a writer. Let your internal editor do his or her work later. You can always clean up sloppy writing afterward. But you can't always tap that creative, uninhibited spirit.

And even though porn writing is all about homework and markets and working hard, it's also about not taking yourself or your market too seriously. Don't let self-doubt or others' opinions sway you now. You're in charge here. For now, all you have to do is enjoy yourself.

Paying Porn Markets

THE AMERICAN SEX SCENE, P.O. Box 731, Hatboro, PA 19025. P(215) 654-9200 F(215) 654-1895 E-mail: Qlimax@aol.com Website: http://www.qlimax.com. CONTACT: Michael Phoenix . True sex story magazine and "Bordello Guide." Reference guides, stories, classifieds and information on sex etiquette covering most of the major cities. Circulation 30,000. 60% freelance written. Works with new writers. Responds "as soon as possible". Buys all rights. Pays on publication. No guidelines. Purchase sample copy online. Submit manuscript via fax or e-mail.

    CURRENT NEEDS: True stories and accounts of the sex scene; bordellos, services, porn stars, etc. Word count varies.

    PAYMENT: No set payment policies

    REPRINTS: Yes, if approved.

    SUBSCRIPTIONS: Single issue - $7.95, 12 issues - $54.95

BABYFACE - 1629 NW 84 Ave, Miami FL 33126. F(305) 662-5952. Website: **http://www.babyfacemag.com**. CONTACT: Joe Monks, editor. Monthly (with occasional holiday issues) young woman magazine which caters to older men who like much younger women. Two or three articles per issue are freelance written. Works with new writers. Responds as soon as possible, faster response via e-mail. Purchases first, world and electronic rights. Pays on publication. Time between acceptance and publication varies. Obtain guidelines via mail or fax. For sample copy, call editorial offices. Submit complete manuscript along with cover letter and SASE.

    CURRENT NEEDS: Fiction and non-fiction work that appeals to an audience that favors young, innocent women and their sexual initiations and experiences.

    PAYMENT: Flat fee decided upon by the editor

    REPRINTS: No

    SUBSCRIPTIONS: US - $49.95 p/year, Mexico and Canada - $64.95 p/year, International - $109.95 p/year

PHOTOS/ART: Pay determined by publisher. BabyFace is always looking for fresh, new talent to contribute. Please send samples and SASE to the editor. Please, for artwork, photocopies only, b/w samples and color samples preferable. No originals, please. Pay determined by publisher

HINTS: BabyFace magazine is looking for hot, erotic fiction that does not overstep the boundaries of good taste. Stories celebrating the joys of sex with young, innocent, just-come-of-legal-age girls, meant to excite the reader, is the goal to keep in mind when writing for BabyFace. Please try to avoid the conventions of the genre and make your submissions vibrant and original, while remaining believable.

BEAU, P.O. Box 170, Irvington NY 10533 - E-mail: DianaEditr@aol.com Website: http://www.youngandtight.com/title.htm CONTACT: Diana Sheridan, Associate Editor. General interest "vanilla" digest for gay males. 100% freelance; some assigned, some unsolicited. Works with new writers. Responds in three weeks, sooner to e-mail submissions. Pays on publication. Time between acceptance and publication "varies greatly." Buys all rights but will reassign book rights on request. Guidelines available online or send SASE. For sample copy send $5.00 and a 6x9 SASE with first-class postage for four ounces. Submit complete manuscript.

CURRENT NEEDS: Doesn't really *need* anything but is always willing to look.

PAYMENT: Pays $100 for a 2,000 – 3,000 word story

REPRINTS: No

PHOTOS/ART: n/a

SUBSCRIPTIONS: U.S - $9.97 for four issues; Canada - $15.97

GUIDELINES: Appear at end of this book

BEST WOMEN'S EROTICA – BWE, 337 17th Street, Oakland, CA 94612. E-mail:marquest@wenet.net CONTACT: Marcy Sheiner, Editor. Book series (published yearly) compiling the best of women's erotica. 10,000 print run. 100% freelance written. Works with new writers. Responds in 2 months. Buys First North American Serial Rights. Pays on acceptance. E-mail marquest@wenet.net for guidelines. Submit typed and double spaced manuscript in hard copy, along with SASE.

CURRENT NEEDS: Erotic stories by women.

PAYMENT:$100 per story

REPRINTS: Yes

GUIDELINES: Appear at end of this book

THE BLOWFISH UPDATE: 3153 16th St., San Francisco CA 94103. E-mail: editor@blowfish.com
Website: http://www.blowfish.com/ CONTACT: Editor. Weekly e-mail newsletter, oriented around the products of Blowfish Mail-Order. "We include one piece of fiction per issue." Fiction is 100% freelance written. Works with new writers. Circulation 10,000. Pays on publication. Pays approximately 2-4 weeks after acceptance. Buys one-time e-mail rights and non-exclusive reprint rights on the web. Responds in 1-4 weeks.

CURRENT NEEDS: Short erotic fiction, maximum of 1,000 words

PAYMENT: $50.00

REPRINTS: Yes

SUBSCRIPTIONS: Free. Send an e-mail message toadd@blowfish.com'

GUIDELINES: online at http://www.blowfish.com/catalog/misc/guidelines.shtml For sample copy write to add@blowfish.com Submit complete manuscript (as a plain text file) in e-mail to editor@blowfish.com. Do not send attachments; they will not be read.

BONDAGE FANTASIES: Bon-Vue Enterprises, P.O. Box 92889, Long Beach, CA 90809-2889. E-Mail: rdante@fs2.bondage.org or margie@fs2.bondage.org Website: http://www.bondage.org. P(310) 631-1600. F(310) 631-0415. CONTACT: Robert Dante, Editor. Quarterly magazine for an adult audience of bondage and discipline, dominance and submission. Magazine includes fiction, drawn artwork and photo features. 85-90% freelance written. Enjoys working with new writers. Responds in two weeks. Purchases all rights. Pays on acceptance. Publishes manuscripts approximately 3 months to 1 year after acceptance.

CURRENT NEEDS: Quality, imaginative fiction featuring female and male dominants with female submissives; explicit, intense, erotic, 1,500-3,000 words.

PAYMENT: Top pay 2.5 ¢ per word OR double this amount in Bon-Vue product (450 BDSM videos in our catalogue).

REPRINTS: No

SUBSCRIPTIONS: $22.00 per year.

PHOTOS/ART: Submit original artwork only; piece is bought outright. Comics and comic strips negotiated. Photos purchased as complete sets, not individual photos. Average pay is $1 per photo.

HINTS: Material that is not acceptable for print publications may be usable on our popular website for a lesser fee. Avoid trite scenarios with lots of sound effects, but be descriptive. Especially looking for work with an "edge" - horror (with bondage, SM), sci-fi (with BDSM), psychological terrorism - - will consider almost anything, except kiddie porn and bestiality. We especially like to work with new writers, but once they've made a sale to us, it's more likely we will work with them again.

GUIDELINES: Appear in this book. Sample copies available upon request. Send complete manuscript with hard copy and disk or send by e-mail. Brief bio helpful. SASE not necessary IF writer does not want to receive story back after submitting.

BOUDOIR NOIR: Bon-Vue Enterprises, P.O. Box 92889, Long Beach, CA 90809-2889. E-Mail: rdante@fs2.bondage.org or margie@fs2.bondage.org Website: http://www.bondage.org. P(310) 631-1600. F(310) 631-0415. CONTACT: Robert Dante, Editor. Bon-Vue Enterprises publishes quarterly magazines for an adult audience of bondage and discipline, dominance and submission.

Magazine includes fiction, non-fiction, drawn artwork and photo features. 85-90% freelance written. Enjoys working with new writers. Responds in two weeks. Purchases ALL rights. Pays on acceptance. Publishes manuscripts approximately 3 months to 1 year after acceptance.

CURRENT NEEDS: Quality, imaginative non fiction and fiction featuring female and male dominants with female submissives; explicit, intense, erotic, 1,500-3,000 words.

PAYMENT: Top pay 2.5 ¢ per word OR double this amount in Bon-Vue product (450 BDSM videos in our catalogue).

REPRINTS: No

SUBSCRIPTIONS: $32.00 per year.

PHOTOS/ART: Submit original artwork only, piece is bought outright. Comics and comic strips negotiated. Photos purchased as complete sets, not individual photos. Average pay is $1 per photo.

HINTS: Material that is not acceptable for print publications may be usable on our popular website for a lesser fee. Avoid trite scenarios with lots of sound effects, but be descriptive. Especially looking for work with an "edge" - horror (with bondage, SM), sci-fi (with BDSM), psychological terrorism - - will consider almost anything, except kiddie porn and bestiality. We especially like to work with new writers, but once they've made a sale to us, it's more likely we will work with them again.

GUIDELINES: Appear in this book. Sample copies available upon request. Send complete manuscript with hard copy and disk or send by e-mail. Brief bio helpful. SASE not necessary IF writer does not want to receive story back after submitting.

BOY NEXT DOOR - PO Box 170, Irvington NY 10533 - E-mail: DianaEditr@aol.com Website: http://www.youngandtight.com/ title.htm CONTACT: Diana Sheridan, Associate Editor. Quarterly "vanilla" digest for gay males. Features guys who are boy-next-door types *and* are in some physical proximity that qualifies as next door (e.g. literal next-door neighbor, guy in the next cube at work or in the office next door, travelling salesman in the next motel room, etc.). 100% freelance; some assigned, some unsolicited. Works with new writers. Responds in three weeks, sooner on E-mail submissions. Pays on publication. Time between acceptance and publication "varies greatly." Buys all rights but will reassign book rights on request.

CURRENT NEEDS: Doesn't really *need* anything but is always willing to look.
PAYMENT: Pays $100 for a 2,000 – 3,000 word story
REPRINTS: No
PHOTOS/ART: n/a
SUBSCRIPTIONS: U.S - $9.97 for four issues; Canada - $15.97
GUIDELINES: Appear in this book. For sample copy send $ 5.00 and a 6x9 SASE with first-class postage for four ounces. Submit complete manuscript.

CHERRY BOYS - PO Box 170, Irvington NY 10533 - E-mail: DianaEditr@aol.com. Website: http://www.youngandtight.com/title.htm CONTACT: Diana Sheridan, Associate Editor. Quarterly "vanilla" digest for gay males about getting a guy's cherry (from the other guy's viewpoint). 100% freelance; some assigned, some unsolicited. Works with new writers. Responds in three weeks, sooner on E-mail submissions. Pays on publication. Time between acceptance and publication "varies greatly." Buys all rights but will reassign book rights on request.

CURRENT NEEDS: Doesn't really *need* anything, but is always willing to look.
PAYMENT: Pays $100 for a 2,000 – 3,000 word story
REPRINTS: No
PHOTOS/ART: n/a
SUBSCRIPTIONS: U.S - $9.97 for four issues; Canada - $15.97
GUIDELINES: Appear at end of this book

CHOCOLATE CREEM - PO Box 170, Irvington NY 10533 E-mail: DianaEditr@aol.com. Website:

http://www.youngandtight.com/title.htm   CONTACT: Diana Sheridan, Associate Editor. Bi-monthly pictorial magazine about African-American girls. Two stories and one feature (not open to freelance submissions) in each issue. 100% freelance; some assigned, some unsolicited. Works with new writers. Responds in three weeks, sooner on E-mail submissions. Pays on publication. Time between acceptance and publication "varies greatly." Buys all rights but will reassign book rights on request. Guidelines available on line or send SASE. For sample copy send $7.00 and a 9x12 SASE with first-class postage for eight ounces. Submit complete manuscript for stories, complete manuscript or queries for articles. Include SASE. Not interested in published clips or resumes, every story or article stands or falls on its own merits.

> CURRENT NEEDS: Doesn't really *need* anything but is always willing to look.
> PAYMENT: Pays $100 for a 2,000 word story
> REPRINTS: No
> PHOTOS/ART: n/a
> SUBSCRIPTIONS: U.S. - $19.97 for 6 issues, Canada - $25.97 f or 6 issues
> HINTS: Read the magazine before you submit, have at least a clue what it is we're looking for
> GUIDELINES: Appear at end of this book

CLEAN SHEETS - E-Mail: editor@cleansheets.com Website: http://www.cleansheets.com – CONTACT: Jaie Helier, Kristine Hawes, Bill Noble / Fiction Editors. Kris Bierk / Poetry Editor. Chris Bridges / Articles Editor. Mary Anne Mohanraj / Editor-in-Chief (general queries) Weekly...Circulation 1,200 hits/day. 20% paid freelance written. Works with new writers. Responds in 1-2 months. Purchases 1st electronic rights and/or ongoing archive rights. Pays "as soon after publication as we can manage." Publishes manuscripts approximately 1-2 months after acceptance.

> CURRENT NEEDS: Quality fiction, poetry, articles and reviews.
> PAYMENT: Fiction: 3 cents/word for new material, 1 cent/word

for reprints. Poetry: $10-20/poem. Nonfiction: Unpaid at present, though we hope to change that soon. Word count varies.
REPRINTS: Yes
PHOTOS/ART: No payment - we feature one artist/month in our gallery.
GUIDELINES: available on-line. Submit complete manuscript with cover letter via e-mail, plain text only.

COMIC FANTASIES: Bon-Vue Enterprises - P.O. Box 92889 - Long Beach, CA 90809-2889. E-Mail: rdante@fs2.bondage.org or margie@fs2.bondage.org Website: http://www.bondage.org. P(310) 631-1600. F(310) 631-0415. CONTACT: Robert Dante, Editor. Bon-Vue Enterprises publishes quarterly magazines for an adult audience of bondage and discipline, dominance and submission. Comic Fantasies material ranges from art portfolios and individual drawings by artists as well as 6-page comic strip stories, sometimes as series with ongoing characters. Enjoys working with new writers. Responds in two weeks. Purchases ALL rights. Pays on acceptance. Publishes manuscripts approximately 3 months to 1 year after acceptance. Guidelines available via e-mail or with SASE. Sample copy available upon request. Send complete manuscript with hard copy and disk or send by e-mail. Brief bio helpful. SASE not necessary IF writer does not want to receive story back after submitting.
CURRENT NEEDS: Quality, imaginative fiction featuring female and male dominants with female submissives; explicit, intense, erotic, PAYMENT: Comics and comic strips negotiated. 1,500-3,000 words.
REPRINTS: No.
SUBSCRIPTIONS: $22.00 per year.
PHOTOS/ART: Submit original artwork only; piece is bought outright.
HINTS: Material that is not acceptable for print publications may be usable on our popular website for a lesser fee. Avoid trite scenarios with lots of sound effects, but be descriptive. Especially

looking for work with an "edge" - horror (with bondage, SM), sci-fi (with BDSM), psychological terrorism - - will consider almost anything, except kiddie porn and bestiality. We especially like to work with new writers, but once they've made a sale to us, it's more likely we will work with them again.
GUIDELINES: Appear at end of this book.

COMING OUT – PO Box 170, Irvington NY 10533 - E-mail: DianaEditr@aol.com. Website: http://www.youngandtight.com/title.htm CONTACT: Diana Sheridan, Associate Editor. Quarterly "vanilla" digest for gay males about a guy's first experience (from his viewpoint). 100% freelance; some assigned, some unsolicited. Works with new writers. Responds in three weeks, sooner on E-mail submissions. Pays on publication. Time between acceptance and publication "varies greatly." Buys all rights but will reassign book rights on request. Guidelines available on line or send SASE. For sample copy send $5.00 and a 6x9 SASE with first-class postage for four ounces. Submit complete manuscript.
    CURRENT NEEDS: Doesn't really *need* anything but is always willing to look.
    PAYMENT: Pays $100 for a 2,000 – 3,000 word story
    REPRINTS: No
    PHOTOS/ART: n/a
    SUBSCRIPTIONS: U.S - $9.97 for four issues; Canada - $15.97
    GUIDELINES: Appear at end of this book.

EROTASY, EXTRAORDINARY EROTIC LITERATURE - PMB 17 - 3145 Geary Blvd. – San Francisco, CA 94118 E-mail: editor@erotasy.com Website: http://www.erotasy.com CONTACT: Louise, Publisher. Erotasy publishes extraordinary erotic literature, has a wildly popular free weekly serial, has free and collectible stories, and is launching a new pay-service that gives free access to the entire site, with bonuses. 95% freelance written. Works with new writers. Responds in 2-6 weeks. Purchases electronic publishing rights, along with print-publishing options. Pays on acceptance.

Posts stories to the website as soon after purchase as possible, usually 1-3 months.

CURRENT NEEDS: We are always looking for quality erotica. Please review our guidelines first. Stories generally run 1,500 to 5,000 words.PAYMENT: $25 to $100 per story.

REPRINTS: Generally not, but occasionally we make exceptions.

SUBSCRIPTIONS: We are developing a "Full Access" program, with free bonuses for $19.99.

HINTS: The most common mistake writers make is not reading our guidelines and reviewing our site.

GUIDELINES: available online http://www.erotasy.com/wguide.shtml. Sample copy available at http://www.erotasy.com. Submit manuscript to http://www.erotasy.com/wguide.shtml.

FETISH BAZAAR: Bon-Vue Enterprises - P.O. Box 92889 - Long Beach, CA 90809-2889. E-Mail: rdante@fs2.bondage.org or margie@fs2.bondage.org Website: http://www.bondage.org. P(310) 631-1600. F(310) 631-0415. CONTACT: Robert Dante, Editor.

Bon-Vue Enterprises publishes quarterly magazines for an adult audience of bondage and discipline, dominance and submission. Magazine includes fiction, drawn artwork and photo features. Fetish Bazaar is similar to Bondage Fantasies but a little more "off the wall. Includes horror and sci-fi." 85-90% freelance written. Enjoys working with new writers. Responds in two weeks. Purchases ALL rights. Pays on acceptance. Publishes manuscripts approximately 3 months to 1 year after acceptance.

CURRENT NEEDS: Quality, imaginative fiction featuring female and male dominants with female submissives; explicit, intense, erotic, 1,500-3,000 words.

PAYMENT: Top pay 2.5 ¢ per word OR double this amount in Bon-Vue product (450 BDSM videos in our catalogue).

REPRINTS: No

SUBSCRIPTIONS: $22.00 per year.

PHOTOS/ART: Submit original artwork only; piece is bought outright. Comics and comic strips negotiated. Photos purchased as complete sets, not individual photos. Average pay is $1 per photo.

HINTS: Material that is not acceptable for print publications may be usable on our popular website for a lesser fee. Avoid trite scenarios with lots of sound effects, but be descriptive. Especially looking for work with an "edge" - horror (with bondage, SM), sci-fi (with BDSM), psychological terrorism - - will consider almost anything, except kiddie porn and bestiality. We especially like to work with new writers, but once they've made a sale to us, it's more likely we will work with them again.

GUIDELINES: available via e-mail or with SASE. Sample copy available upon request. Send complete manuscript with hard copy and disk or send by e-mail. Brief bio helpful. SASE not necessary IF writer does not want to receive story back after submitting.

GUIDELINES: Appear at end of this book.

GENESIS MAGAZINE – 210 Route 4 East, Suite 401, Paramus NJ 07652.P(201)843-4004.F(201)843-8636.
E-mail: Genesismag@aol.com Website: www.genesismagazine.com
CONTACT – Dan Davis, Managing Editor. Monthly adult publication featuring celebrity interviews; topical, adult-themed features and erotic fiction and non-fiction. Circulation 450,000. 90% written. Works with new writers. Responds in 4-6 weeks. Buys first and second world wide rights. Pays on publication. Publishes manuscripts 3-6 months after acceptance.

CURRENT NEEDS: Non-fiction, celebrity interviews
PAYMENT: Varies - $.22 p/word up to $1,500.00 p/article.
REPRINTS: Yes
PHOTOS/ART: Send slides, pays per article.
SUBSCRIPTIONS: U.S. – 13 issues/$34.07. Canada – 13 issues/ $34.97. All others – 13 issues/$42.00
HINTS: Mainly seeking non-fiction and celebrity interviews.

GUIDELINES: E-mail for guidelines or send SASE. Sample copy available for $6.99. Submit complete manuscript or query with bio, cover letter and SASE. Prefers hard copy for queries and manuscripts.

GUIDELINES: Appear at end of this book.

GENT - 14411 Commerce Way, Suite 420, Miami Lakes, FL 33016. Website: http://www.sexmags.com. CONTACT: Fritz Bailey. Monthly adult magazine slanted towards men who like big breasts - "Home of the D-Cups!" Circulation 100,000. Fiction and interviews are freelance written, features generally done by regulars. Works with new writers. Responds in three months. Buys first and electronic rights. "Every story we publish also goes up on our website, so we're also buying perpetual electronic rights when we buy your story. If the thought of your story on our site bothers you, please don't bother submitting." Pays on publication. Time between acceptance and publication varies, "We get many submissions, so please be patient." Send complete manuscript. For sample copy send a written request and a check for $7.00. For guidelines send SASE.

CURRENT NEEDS: We're fairly well stocked, but we're always willing to look at new erotic fiction and/or letters. Fiction length 2,500 words.

PAYMENT: Fiction pays $250 for 2500 word story. Letters pay $100 1,000 words, $150 for 1,500 words etc.

REPRINTS: Not for fiction, maybe for interviews

PHOTOS/ART: Send SASE for photo guidelines

SUBSCRIPTION: U.S. – 13 issues/$46.00, Canada and overseas – 13 issues/$59.00

HINTS: Forget cover letter nonsense, we don't care about it. Just write a good story. A story that flows well, makes sense, fits our word requirements, and most importantly will turn people on. Don't be afraid to be filthy, and don't waste too much time on exposition. It's a sex story, not a novel.

HEROTICA 7 - Down There Press, 938 Howard Street, San

Francisco, CA 94103. CONTACT: Leigh Davidson, Manager.
Seventh in a series of books on women's erotica. Published every
two years. This edition will be on the theme of multi-cultural
relationships. 25,000 print run. 100% freelance written. Works with
new writers. Responds in three months. Buys First North American
Serial Rights. Pays on acceptance. Publishes manuscript one-two
years after acceptance.

    CURRENT NEEDS: Erotic stories by women on theme
of cross-cultural relationships. No more than 20 pages.
PAYMENT: $15.00 per page plus royalties
REPRINTS: No
GUIDELINES: E-mail GoodVibrations@well.com or
marquest@wenet.net For sample copy try Amazon.com or any
bookstore. Submit typed and double spaced manuscript in hard
copy, along with SASE and bio.
GUIDELINES: Appear at end of this book.

HOT LATINAS - PO Box 170, Irvington, NY 10533 – E-mail:
DianaEditr@aol.com. Website: http://www.youngandtight.com/
title.htm. CONTACT: Diana Sheridan, Associate Editor Quarterly
pictorial magazine about Latina girls. Includes stories and one
feature (feature not open for submissions). 100% freelance; some
unsolicited, some assigned. Works with new writers. Responds in
three weeks, sooner on E-mail submissions. Pays on publication.
Time between acceptance and publication "varies greatly." Buys all
rights but will reassign book rights on request. Guidelines available on
line or send SASE. For sample copy send $7.00 and a 9x12 SASE with
first-class postage for eight ounces. Submit complete manuscript.

    CURRENT NEEDS: Doesn't really *need* anything but is
always willing to look.
PAYMENT: Pays $100 per 2,000 word story
REPRINTS: No
PHOTOS/ART: n/a
SUBSCRIPTIONS: U.S. - $19.97 for 6 issues, Canada –
$25.97 for 6 issuesHINTS: Read the magazine before you

submit, have at least a clue what it is we're looking for
GUIDELINES: Appear at end of this book.

JUST 18 - 210 Route 4 East - Suite 401 - Paramus, NJ 07652. CONTACT: Odette Diaz, Managing Editor. Sexually oriented men's magazine with a focus on younger women (18-20 years). Published monthly. Circulation 100,000. 75% freelance written. Welcomes new writers. Pays on publication. Responds in 30-60 days. Publishes manuscripts approximately 3-4 months after acceptance. Buys first rights. For guidelines send SASE. For sample copy send $6.95 payable to Swank Publications. Submit complete manuscript by mail with SASE.

    CURRENT NEEDS: Fiction catering to the interests of men who prefer younger women. Letters are 1,000 words and short fiction is 2,500-3,000 words.
    PAYMENT: Pays $0.13 per word
    REPRINTS: No
    HINTS: "When attempting to write erotica, some writers forget that it's still important for the story to have a beginning, a middle, and an end. Character is also important. It's not enough to just say a girl is 18. She should also act it.

LAMBDA BOOK REPORT - PO Box 73910 - Washington, DC 20056. P(202) 462-7924. F(202) 462-5264. E-mail: lbreditor@aol.com. Website: http://www.lambdalit.org. CONTACT: Shelley Bindon, Editor. Monthly review of glbt (gay, lesbian, bisexual and transgender) books and literature, serving as a forum for news and issues in the glbt publishing industry. Circulation 4500. 90% freelance written. Works with new writers, but only with "clips and a c.v. or an introduction from an established writer." Pays 60 days after publication. Response time is immediate. Publishes ms. within 60 days. Buys first print publication and first electronic rights.

    CURRENT NEEDS: Book reviews.
    PAYMENT: $10 - $75 depending on assignment for 30-2900 words.

REPRINTS: No

PHOTOS/ART: Book authors. Pays $0-$20 depending on photo.

SUBSCRIPTIONS: $29.95/yr U.S. - $58.95/yr overseas

HINTS: "We only review glbt books."

GUIDELINES: available via e-mail. Sample copies available by purchasing a back issue or newsstand issue. Submit using procedure in writer's guidelines.

LEG SEX - 629 NW 84th Ave - Miami, Fl 33126. F(305) 662-5952. E-mail: legsexedtr@aol.com Website: http://www.legsex.com. CONTACT: Joe Monks, editor. Bi-monthly magazine devoted to the leg and foot man, featuring the most beautiful women with the hottest legs on the planet. 90% freelance written. Works with new writers. Pays on publication. Responds in 4 weeks. Time between acceptance and publication varies. Buys First World Rights.

REPRINTS: No

PAYMENT: Varies depending on story or article or column, freelance or assignment. $50 and up for reader confessions, $200-400 for features. Length for both fiction and articles: 2,400 to 4,000 words

PHOTOS/ART: Photographs of great legs are always welcome, amateur or professional, single images, sequential layouts both welcome. Payment varies, between $1,000 and $1,800 for single girl, rates depend on length of usage in magazine, hardcore/softcore, single girl/multiple girl/boy-girl.

HINTS: Submit manuscripts and/or queries AFTER December 2000.

GUIDELINES: Send query via e-mail to editor for guidelines. To submit, send query letter via e-mail or snail mail with brief synopsis of story concept.

OCEANIA LIMITED – E-mail: oceania@peacockblue.com Website: http://www.peacockblue.com. CONTACT: Oceania. Oceania is a company that creates and produces audio stories for

adult webmasters. Enjoys working with new writers. Responds in
10 days. Author keeps all rights except for a 60 day exclusive before
work is submitted/printed anywhere else. Pays within 30 days of
acceptance. E-mail first to see what themes are needed, then follow
up with a sample.

CURRENT NEEDS: Looking for writers that can write fetish
work for adult webmasters. Stories must be 500-750 words with
plot, lust, hunger. Serials and continuing stories accepted.
PAYMENT: Pays 1.5 cents p/word up to 750 words and $1.00
per story royalty when it goes into distribution
REPRINTS: No
PHOTOS/ART: Submit in jpg format, contact for payment info.
HINTS: The ones that find me are so talented, so inventive and
so scared in the beginning that I will reject their work. So it
is not what a writer puts in their cover letter it is what they let
an editor see of their soul.
GUIDELINES: By e-mail.

OPTIONS - PO Box 170, Irvington NY 10533 - E-mail:
DianaEditr@aol.com. Website: http://www.youngandtight.com/
title.htm CONTACT: Diana Sheridan, Associate Editor. Published
ten times per year. Digest magazine for bisexuals. 100% freelance;
stories and articles are open to freelancers. Works with new writers.
Responds in three weeks, sooner on E-mail submissions. Pays
on publication. Time between acceptance and publication "varies
greatly." Buys all rights but will reassign book rights on request.

CURRENT NEEDS: Looking for serious articles – there is one
in each issue - but is willing to look at hot stories too
PAYMENT: Pays $100 for a 2,000 – 3,000 word story
REPRINTS: No
PHOTOS/ART: n/a
SUBSCRIPTIONS: U.S. - $9.97, Canada – 15.97
HINTS: Read the magazine before you submit, have at least a
clue what it is we're looking for.
GUIDELINES: available on line or send SASE. For sample copy

send $2.95 and a 6x9 SASE with first-class postage for four ounces. Submit complete manuscript for stories, complete manuscript or queries for articles. Include SASE. Not interested in published clips or resumes, every story or article stands or falls on its own merits.
GUIDELINES: Appear at end of this book.

PETITE - 14411 Commerce Way, Suite 420, Miami Lakes, FL 33016. Website: http://www.sexmags.com. CONTACT: Fritz Bailey.
Bi-monthly adult magazine slanted towards men who like younger women, in the tradition of magazines like Barely Legal and Hawk. Circulation 50,000. Fiction and interviews are freelance written, features generally done by regulars. Works with new writers. Responds in three months. Buys first and electronic rights. "Every story we publish also goes up on our website, so we're also buying perpetual electronic rights when we buy your story. If the thought of your story on our site bothers you, please don't bother submitting." Pays on publication. Time between acceptance and publication varies, "We get many submissions, so please be patient." Send complete manuscript. For sample copy send a written request and a check for $7.00. For guidelines send SASE.
CURRENT NEEDS: We're fairly well stocked, but we're always willing to look at new erotic fiction and/or letters. Fiction length – 2,500 words.
PAYMENT: Fiction pays $250 for 2500 word story. Letters pay $100.
REPRINTS: No
PHOTOS/ART: Send SASE for photo guidelines
SUBSCRIPTION: U.S. – 6 issues/$21.00, Canada and overseas – 6 issues/$27.00
HINTS: Forget cover letter nonsense, we don't care about it. Just write a good story that flows well, makes sense, fits our word requirements, and most importantly will turn people on. Don't be afraid to be filthy, and don't waste too much time on exposition. It's a sex story, not a novel.

QLIMAX TIMES - P.O. Box 731 - Hatboro, PA 19025. P(215) 654-9200 F(215) 654-1895 E-mail: Qlimax@aol.com Website: http://www.qlimax.com. CONTACT: Michael Phoenix .
Erotic news oriented newspaper in a tabloid format. Covers the major cities in the U.S. in erotic form. Circulation 30,000. 60% freelance written. Works with new writers. Responds "as soon as possible". Buys all rights. Pays on publication. No guidelines. Purchase sample copy online. Submit manuscript via fax or e-mail.
    CURRENT NEEDS: True stories and accounts of the sex scene; bordellos, services, porn stars, etc. Word count varies.
    PAYMENT: No set payment policies
    REPRINTS: Yes, if approved.
    SUBSCRIPTIONS: Single issue - $4.95, 12 issues - $44.95

SWANK – 210 Route 4 East - Ste 401 – Paramus NJ 07652. P(201)843-4004. F(201)843-8636 or F(201)843-8775. E-mail: Genesismag@aol.com Website: swankmag.com CONTACT: David Dezuzio, Associate Editor. Monthly magazine of men's adult entertainment. Circulation 320,000. 75% freelance written. Works with new writers. Responds in 1-5 months. Buys 1st rights. Pays on publication.
    CURRENT NEEDS: Adult oriented fiction, non-fiction and how-to's. No more than 1,000 words – 1,500 for features.
    PAYMENT: $.22 per word
    REPRINTS: Yes
    PHOTOS/ART: Send in chromes. No instant photos, no digital photos.
    SUBSCRIPTIONS: 1 year: US - $34.97, Canada - $42.00, All Others - $60.00
    HINTS: We need plenty of "How-to's". Send full articles, not brief write-ups.
    GUIDELINES: Request guidelines via regular mail or e-mail. For sample copy send check. Submit complete manuscript along with SASE.

YOUNG & TIGHT - PO Box 170, Irvington NY 10533 - E-mail: DianaEditr@aol.com. Website: http://www.youngandtight.com/ title.htm CONTACT: Diana Sheridan, Associate Editor. Published eight times a year. Pictorial magazine about 18 and 19 year old girls. One story and one feature in each issue. The feature is "Ambisexters' Club" and purports to tell the story of a bi girl. 100% freelance; some unsolicited, some assigned. Works with new writers. Responds in three weeks, sooner on E-mail submissions. Pays on publication. Time between acceptance and publication "varies greatly." Buys all rights but will reassign book rights on request.

  CURRENT NEEDS: Doesn't really *need* anything but is always willing to look

  PAYMENT: Pays $100 for 2,000 word story, $50 for 1000 word "Ambixexters' Club" feature

  REPRINTS: No

  PHOTOS/ART: n/a

  SUBSCRIPTIONS: U.S. - $19.97 for eight issues, Canada - $25.97 for eight issues

  HINTS: Read the magazine before you submit, have at least a clue what it is we're looking for

  GUIDELINES: available on-line or send SASE. For sample copy send $7.00 and a 9x12 SASE with first-class postage for eight ounces. Submit complete manuscript.

  GUIDELINES: Appear at end of this book.

YOUNG & TIGHT FANTASIES - PO Box 170, Irvington NY 10533 - E-mail: DianaEditr@aol.com. Website: http://www.youngandtight.com/title.htm CONTACT: Diana Sheridan, Associate Editor. Quarterly (soon to increase in frequency) heterosexual digest. Contains long "letters" and one story. 100% freelance; some unsolicited, some assigned. Works with new writers. Responds in three weeks, sooner on E-mail submissions. Pays on publication. Time between acceptance and publication "varies greatly". Buys all rights but will reassign book rights on request.

CURRENT NEEDS: Doesn't really *need* anything but is always willing to look

PAYMENT: Pays $20 per 1,000 word letter; $100 per 2000 word story

REPRINTS: No

PHOTOS/ART: n/a

HINTS: Read the magazine before you submit, have at least a clue what it is we're looking for

GUIDELINES: available on-line or send SASE. For sample copy send $5.00 and a 6x9 SASE with first-class postage for four ounces. Submit complete manuscript.

GUIDELINES: Appear at end of this book.

Non-Paying Porn Markets

BATTERIES NOT INCLUDED - 130 W. Limestone - Yellow Springs OH 45387. P(937) 767-7416. E-mail: BNI@AOL.COM CONTACT: Richard Freeman, Publisher. Monthly "politically incorrect newsletter on the Sexual Underground". 100% free-lance written. Works with new writers. Responds in 1 day for e-mail, 1 week for post office. Publishes manuscripts approximately 3 months after acceptance. No guidelines. For sample copy send $3. Submit complete manuscript.

> CURRENT NEEDS: Non fiction writing on classic pornography. Amusing writing on human sexuality. No minimum/maximum word counts.
> REPRINTS: Yes
> SUBSCRIPTIONS: $36 U.S. - $48 Foreign
> PHOTOS/ART: No photos
> HINTS: Please do not send fiction or poetry, Batteries Not Included is non-fiction only

EIDOS - PO Box 96 - Boston, MA 02137-0096 – E-mail: eidos@eidos.org Website: http://www.eidos.org P(617) 262-0096. F(617) 364-0096. CONTACT: Brenda Loew, Editor. EIDOS is an acronym for Everyone Is Doing Outrageous Sex. We are an upscale, quarterly independent pansexual erotic lifestyle and entertainment magazine for freethinking consenting adults who value sexual freedom and their first amendment and personal privacy rights. Circulation 18,000. 100% freelance written. Works with new writers. Responds in 6 - 8 weeks. Buys First North American Serial Rights. Pays on publication. Publishes manuscripts 4 - 12 months after acceptance.

> CURRENT NEEDS: Fiction and nonfiction, 500 to 2,500 words. We don't need poetry right now.
> PAYMENT: Contributor Copies
> REPRINTS: No.

SUBSCRIPTIONS: 4 issues: North America – US $25, Europe – US $31, All Others - US $33

HINTS: We are not interested in seeing handwritten submissions, material that has been submitted elsewhere, manuscripts with typos or material that is clearly inappropriate for EIDOS. We are a very unique niche magazine. It is wise to be familiar with our publication before submitting material. We prefer considering material that is sent to us on a floppy disk accompanied by a hard copy print out.

GUIDELINES: For guidelines send #10 SASE. For sample copy send $5. Submit complete manuscript (good, clean copy) and floppy disk (preferred), cover letter, bio and SASE by mail.

NOT QUITE A WEBZINE: E-mail: oceania@peacockblue Website: http://www.peacockblue.com CONTACT: Oceania. Monthly online magazine of written erotica with plot, characters and passion. 75% freelance written. Enjoys working with new writers. Responds in 10 days. Author keeps all rights. Publishes manuscripts approximately 2 months after acceptance. Request guidelines via e-mail. Before submitting, e-mail first to see what themes are needed, then follow up with a sample.

CURRENT NEEDS: Short stories, poetry, art, photos. No word limits.

PAYMENT: Does not pay yet.

REPRINTS: Yes

PHOTOS/ART: Submit in jpg format.

HINTS: "Not Quite A Webzine is a magazine that showcases talent. It doesn't just talk to women. It doesn't talk high above the heads of the readers. It is a place to let out a scream that erotica has a place in life, all lives. That it is the essence of life and should not be hidden. That it is not an anatomy lesson or for Pavlov's dogs. It requires thought."

WRITER'S GUIDELINES

BEAU, COMING OUT, BOY NEXT DOOR, CHERRY BOYS

BEAU, COMING OUT, BOY NEXT DOOR, and CHERRY BOYS are magazines for and about gay men. Our stories are all written in the first person, as if true. If the name of the person telling the story is mentioned in the story (such as if another character calls him by name), the by-line must match that name. If you sell to us repeatedly, please change the by-line from story to story. We cannot have "John Doe" as a fireman one issue, a sailor the next, 34 years old one issue and 18 the next, etc.

Story length is 2000-3000 words (typically 8-12 manuscript pages). You must get into the hot action after no more than 1000 words' exposition (or sooner) and sustain the heat through fully half the manuscript (or more). Please indicate your word count on the manuscript. Please conform your terminology for body parts-if you use the word "cock," make it "cock" consistently throughout the story; or use "dick" or "prick" instead, but whichever you choose, be consistent. Generic words such as "rod" or "tool" may be alternated for variety if desired.

Payment is $100, on publication. We do pay promptly and report on submissions within a few weeks. We buy all rights but will reassign book rights on request after your story has been published. Any stories sent us are automatically considered for all our magazines, including our bisexual magazine, OPTIONS.

For **BOY NEXT DOOR**: The "boy" must be of age though young, must be a "boy-next-door" type, and must be in some physical proximity that could qualify in the large sense as "next door"-e.g. occupant of the next office, next campsite, etc.

Stories set in the AIDS era (1980 on) must depict safe sex only, whether it is condom use, "on me, not in me," mutual j/o, thigh-fucking, etc. Otherwise the story must be clearly set back pre-AIDS. We do not consider unprotected oral sex to be safe sex, even if the character withdraws before ejaculation. We will accept as "safe sex" unprotected sex between two totally monogamous partners who have been negative-tested if that situation is made very explicit.

All four magazines are distributed in Canada. Canadian censorship restrictions make the following things taboo: underage (must be 18 or over), incest (including sex between relatives not related by blood, e.g. in-laws or step-relatives), golden showers and scat, degradation or humiliation, B&D, S&M, rape, bestiality, and a few other things you're not likely to write about. Additionally, we will not accept material depicting use of any drug or involving members of the clergy.

Submissions on disk are encouraged, but please include hard copy as well. We also gladly accept electronic submissions. You can also contact us online at: DianaEditr@aol.com Please note that this online address is only good for the editorial department. We will not consider simultaneous submissions-there is no need; we report promptly, usually within three weeks.

We are not buying "letters" at this time.

For **BEAU** only, we also will consider submissions for our "Gay Style" feature. This is nonfiction; the range of topic is broad. Among the topics we have used in the past have included politics, gay stereotypes, relationships, film, theatre, and TV, cooking, vacationing, book reviews, body building, fashion, and music. We are presently particularly interested in politically oriented or issue-oriented themes, but remember the time lag involved in publishing and don't send us anything that will be stale or outdated by the time it's published. We strongly suggest for your own sake that you query first on "Gay Style" submissions but are happy to look at finished manuscripts. However, we do not offer kill fees, and if we give you a go-ahead on a topic, you are still writing on spec.

COMING OUT and **CHERRY BOYS** are about a man's first man-to-man sexual experience. Stories in COMING OUT are told from the point of view of the first-timer.

Stories in CHERRY BOYS are told from the point of view of the guy who gets the cherry. In all our magazines, a character portrayed as "cherry" should demonstrate some emotional reaction (e.g. fear, excitement) to the step he contemplates taking.

BEST WOMENS EROTICA GUIDELINES

Cleis Press is launching an exciting new series of the best of women's erotica. The first edition is scheduled for publication in March 2000. Marcy Sheiner, editor of Herotica 4, 5 and 6 (Down There Press) and The Oy of Sex: Jewish Women Write Erotica (Cleis) will be choosing the selections. M.J. Rose, author of the novel Lip Service, which made publishing history when it was bought by Pocket Books after first being published on the Internet, will serve as judge.

We're seeking fresh new voices that illustrate what people have been reading and writing during the past year, whether on the Internet, in zines, or in mainstream fiction. Previously published material will be considered as well as never-before-seen stories.

The criteria for a great erotic story are: plot and character development; hot sex; superb writing; and substance. Tell us your wildest fantasies and experiences; how different sexual situations affect you; some stunning insights about human nature you've gleaned beneath the sheets (or on the kitchen table, floor, or on a subway!)

Send stories no longer than twenty pages, double-spaced, with SASE and contact info (e-mail if you have it) to: BWE, Marcy

Sheiner, 337 17th Street, Oakland, CA 94612. Payment will be in the range of $100 per story. Deadline is November 1st of every year.

BON-VUE ENTERPRISES
WRITER'S GUIDELINES

For nearly 20 years, Bill Majors' Bon-Vue Enterprises (B&D Pleasures) has produced and distributed the best in BDSM magazines and videos. Bon-Vue is currently filming four original videos every month and now has nearly 450 bondage, SM and fetish videos in its catalogue. With four regular publication and a burgeoning worldwide web site, we constantly seek new and fresh talent and material. As a small publisher (15,000 copies readership), we cannot compete with Hustler or Penthouse — so we try to compensate by giving artists and writers artistic freedom (unique in the publishing industry!) and a friendly relationship which includes in-kind compensation (see Compensation below). We want cutting-edge stories, photos and artwork. If you'll bring your talent and kinky imagination to Bon-Vue —we'll help you to reach your audience and obtain self-satisfaction! Call us if you have questions — while you won't get rich, you can have fun!

BON-VUE ENTERPRISES
http://www.bondage.org
901 W. Victoria, Unit G, Compton CA 90220
p(310) 631-1600
Rdante@fs2.bondage.org
Bmajors@cyberverse.com
F(310) 631-0415

CONTRIBUTOR'S GUIDELINES

BONDAGE FANTASIES, FETISH BAZAAR

Original fiction only. No reprints. Stories highlighting dominant male- submissive female BDSM interactions, featuring bondage and discipline, fetishes, corporal punishment, sadomasochism, sexual extremes. Stories with plots preferred, but the emphasis should be on the action. The more wicked, the better! Torture, humiliation, degradation not only okay but desired. Incest is okay, but pedophilia is absolutely forbidden. Stories run 1,000-2,500 words, submitted in hard copy, by modem/fax or by disk or e-mail. Each issue features three to four stories. Bon-Vue reserves the right to illustrate and/or to edit submissions. Bon-Vue purchases all rights to a story in perpetuity. Note: Original material is also purchased for use on our popular worldwide web site.

BOUDOIR NOIR

Query first! Original, high quality nonfiction only. The magazine considers leather-fetish-consensual S&M to be a sexual orientation of a large but discreet audience, and writers should view their material as part of a healthy and imaginative sexual lifestyle, regardless of genders of the participants or their gender preferences. No sensationalism. Stories run 1,500-3,000 words, submitted in writing, by modem/fax or by disk. Each issue has an interview or profile, a look at a Scene-related issue, a "how-to" if the source has credentials. We do look at specific fetishes if author is sensitive to the "inner trip" and can clearly communicate it. Bon-Vue purchases all rights to a story in perpetuity. No depictions or descriptions of scat, blood, bestiality, anything which smacks of pedophilia or "degradation" (a strange concept). Bon-Vue reserves the right to edit stories.

Photographers

Domination is the name of the game in our photographs. We're looking for "The Edge" - - fear, intensity, sexuality, raw and savage passion. Bondage, gags, SM, fetish. Fem dom okay, male dom preferred, subs are primarily young females, rarely male subs. No sexual penetration for the U.S. market, however some penetration may be depicted for the European market. Signed releases and copies of photo IDs from all models must be obtained (send for our package which includes our copyrighted standard releases). All models must be 18 years of age with legal proof and there are additional requirements in accordance with federal law. Bon-Vue purchases, keeps and owns the negatives and all rights to the images in perpetuity. Submit digital photos on Zip disk or by e-mail as an attachment. Bon-Vue purchases entire sets of photos, not individual photographs. Photographer will be required to make assurance to Bon-Vue that photo sets are unique and complete (in other words, photos taken at a specific photo shoot should be for Bon-Vue alone).

Artists

Original artwork only. It is our philosophy that fine art allows the viewing public to experience things which could never happen in real life or to depict scenes that can occur in real life but from the unique perspective of the artist. As with photos, explicit nudity and BDSM sexuality increases the chances of being accepted. However, unlike photos, sexual penetration is okay. We're looking for "The Edge," feel free to let your fantasies and dreams come true in your artwork. Let your kinky imagination soar! Bon-Vue purchases and owns the artwork itself. Special deals negotiated for entire comic stories. Most media, sizes acceptable.

Compensation

Rates are determined by staff on per-case basis based on quality, size/length, where it will appear, market value and budget for current projects. While payment is not large, a payment alternative allows the contributor to select twice the dollar equivalent in product from Bon-Vue's extensive catalogue of BDSM publications and videos. Special rates negotiated for entire collections of stories, photos and complete illustrated comic stories. Call us for details — we are happy to speak with you personally because we are certain that we can learn from each other.

CHOCOLATE CREEM GUIDELINES

Stories for Chocolate Creem should be 2000 words and get to the heat within 500 words, sustaining the heat for the rest of the story except for perhaps one paragraph or so of wrap-up at the end. Stories should be about a black woman in a sexual encounter with either a black or white man. Story may be told either from the gal's viewpoint or the guy's. All stories/features are written in the first person, as if true.

The "Wild Ebonee" column is regularly assigned to one writer and is not open to freelance submissions.

Please pick one name per body part (pussy/cunt/cunny, dick/ prick/cock) per story and stick to it throughout.

The magazine is distributed in Canada, so please observe the Canadian censorship taboos, which include B&D, S&M, menstrual sex, sex with a pregnant woman, golden showers, incest, spanking, dominance, humiliation, degradation, rape, bestiality, and underage. In addition to the Canadian taboos, we also do not want references to clergy or to any drugs.

Pay is $100 per story, payable on publication. We do not consider simultaneous submissions; we respond very promptly, normally within three weeks, so there is no reason to submit elsewhere at the same time. Submissions may be made in the form of hardcopy, preferably with a disk enclosed, or as an attached textfile via E-mail. SASE must be enclosed for notification (and return of disk) even if manuscript is disposable.

If submitting or corresponding by e-mail, the address is: DianaEditr@aol.com

GENESIS GUIDELINES

EROTIC FICTION

All erotic fiction ("Forum letters included) currently being used by *Genesis* must follow certain legal guidelines. It is a federal felony to discuss or even insinuate that any person involved in a sexual act is under the age of 18. This includes talking about any sexual act they might have done before the person turned 18. No copy will be accepted or paid for that does not strictly adhere to this rule.

Genesis is distributed in Canada, and the censors there practice their own strict standards regarding sexual material. To avoid problems, we shy away from material we think they may object to. Thus we cannot consider stories about, or containing, the following:

1) S & M (including light bondage and mild humiliation)
2) Unconscious, or dead, participants in sexual acts
3) Incest
4) Bestiality
5) Any sexual scene that states or insinuates pain or the use of force

GIRL COPY

Girl copy for *Genesis* is to follow the theme of the layout it will accompany, in some way, shape or form. Always vary the plots and your writing patterns for piece assigned, as often, the same writer will be featured in an issue more than once, and we want each piece to sound as if it were written by the individual girls. Also, try to include "quotes" from the girls, refer their appearance as best as possible, and not repeat scenarios. Please look over the latest issue of *Genesis* to see what has been done, and adjust your ideas accordingly. A sample copy is available for $6.99 postpaid; please make checks or money orders payable to *Genesis* Publications.

NON-FICTION

All non-fiction submitted must be accompanied by footnotes and references. Do not include children in any articles, unless previously discussed. Reviews that are written must have accompanying artwork submitted with the copy, unless previously discussed.

STYLE

Adhere to the following basic style points when typing your manuscript:

1) Do not indent paragraphs-merely hit return
2) One space after a period
3) There are no spaces before or after an em-dash
4) Movie, video, book, publication and album titles are italicized
5) Song, article and TV show names are in quotes
6) In titles, each word has initial caps
7) Punctuation is always inside the quotes
8) Numbers one through ten are always written out
9) Single quotes are used inside of a conversation as in an interview

When finished, please proof your manuscript. Also, be sure to spell check. Check all uses of tenses. In erotic fiction, make sure the acts depicted are actually possible and in the correct sequence. Make sure all assigned word counts are adhered to.

PROCEDURE

Queries and submissions are to be typed double-space and accompanied by a SASE. In most cases, we respond to article queries within three weeks, and manuscripts within five weeks. To expedite matters, please also include a computer disk with the article saved as text. Due to the volume of material we receive, we discourage phone calls an faxed queries/submissions.

Final submissions must be sent in one of two formats:

1) An IBM or Macintosh computer disk with the article saved as a text file
2) Via e-mail at Genesismag@aol.com. Either attach a text file or the file in which the piece was written (preferred), or copy and paste your article into E-mail's message field.

TERMS

Payment is upon publication. You will be notified of the publication date and rate of pay after acceptance. All articles paid by length are according to the final edit. An invoice must be submitted with any accepted or assigned copy with the author's social security number in order for payment to be made.

HEROTICA 7 GUIDELINES

We're gathering material for our annual collection of woman-authored and focused erotica. In Herotica 7 we'll focus on a multicultural approach: Is your heritage Navajo, Iraqui, Swiss? Israeli, Chilean or Inuit? Whatever your ethnic or cultural background, how has it affected your sex life, solo or partnered? Are you a first, second, third (or more)-generation immigrant? Have you been involved with someone from another race/culture? If so, what were the effects, positive or negative, of cultural differences on the sex in these encounters/relationships? What did you learn from one another? What issues did you struggle with? How did you work them out? We're looking for stories of substance that illustrate how ethnic or cultural differences get played out in the bedroom.

We welcome revelations that go beyond the experience of the young, the hip, the white and/or the middle class, with characters of all sexual orientations who relish all aspects of the sexual imagination. We're looking for arousing, unpredictable stories with strong narrative qualities that reflect the variety, detail and adventure of women's sexuality and that focus on the woman's pleasure.

This volume of Herotica will be edited by Marcy Sheiner, a contributor to the first three volumes and the editor of Herotica 4, 5 and 6. Mary Anne Mohanraj, contributor to Herotica 6 and author of Torn Shapes of Desire, will serve as Consulting Editor. Contributors will receive initial and ongoing payments for their stories, depending on sales, and a share of any subsidiary rights sold.

The Herotica series has been acknowledged by The Nation as "representing images of desire for the nineties." Kirkus Reviews describe it as "the most successful series so far of erotica written by women." Other mentions have appeared in numerous publications, including the New York Times, USA Today, SF Chronicle, Whole Earth Review, Playboy, and Publishers Weekly.

Send stories to Down There Press, Attn: HER, 938 Howard St., San Francisco, CA 94103. Submissions must be typed and double-spaced and include author's name, address and phone number, as well as a SASE.

HOT LATINAS GUIDELINES

Stories for *Hot Latinas* should be 2000 words and get to the heat within 500 words, sustaining the heat for the rest of the story except for perhaps one paragraph or so of wrap-up at the end. Stories should be about a Latina girl, preferably young but at least 18. We will buy some stories of Latinas with Anglo guys, some of Latinas with Latino guys, and a few girl/girl stories as well. We are not at this time contemplating stories of Latinas with black non-Latinos, but I will not rule it out for all time. Story may be told from either viewpoint—girl's or guy's.

All stories/features are written in the first person, as if true.

If you are familiar with "Spanglish," or a smattering of Spanish, please use just a few Spanglish or Spanish words where appropriate, but not too heavily. Since our readers are both Latinos and non-Latinos, do not use Spanish words in places where comprehending them is crucial to understanding the story, so our non-Spanish-speaking readers don't have trouble understanding the story. If you are not conversant with the language, please don't try and fall on your face.

Please pick one name per body part (pussy/cunt/cunny, dick/prick/cock) per story and stick to it throughout.

The magazine is distributed in Canada, so please observe the Canadian censorship taboos, which include B&D, S&M, menstrual sex, sex with a pregnant woman, golden showers, incest, spanking, dominance, humiliation, degradation, rape, bestiality, and underage. In addition to the Canadian taboos, we also do not want references to clergy or to *any* drugs.

Pay is $100 for stories, payable on publication. The column "Angelina, la Diabla" is regularly assigned to one writer and not open for freelance submissions. We do not consider simultaneous submissions; we respond very promptly, normally within three weeks, so there is no reason to submit elsewhere at the same time. Submissions may be made in the form of hardcopy, preferably with a disk enclosed, or as an attached textfile via e-mail. SASE must be enclosed for notification (and return of disk) even if manuscript is disposable.

If submitting or corresponding by e-mail, the address is: DianaEditr@aol.com. We welcome submissions by e-mail, and you'll get a faster answer this way. Be sure to supply your realworld address too in case we accept your story and need to mail a contract and later a check.

OPTIONS GUIDELINES

All stories for Options should be about sex between two (or occasionally more) men or two (or occasionally more) women. We very seldom use threesome stories mixing both sexes. Best advice: Don't send us one. Length should be about 2000-3000 words (usually 8-12 typed, d/s pages). We use material about both sexes but use more male/male than female/female. Hot first-person stories should sound real, whether or not they are. The by-line should match the name of the character telling the story, if his/her name is mentioned. We use more hot, first-person stories than anything else but do run one serious (or serio-comic) piece in each issue, which should not be ponderous and/or boring. Humor is also welcome. We also have one slot in each issue for material that doesn't fit either format, if it's good. Please indicate your manuscript's word count.

Get to the hot action by 1000 words into the manuscript (sooner is fine!). Sustain the heat for at least half the story.

Though most of our readership is presumably bi, our readers are not buying Options to read about male-female sex. They can get that from many other magazines. What they want to read about in Options is the gay side of bisexuality. Consequently, almost none of our articles/stories include male-female sex. You may indicate the viewpoint character's bisexuality by saying that he is or once was married, or has or has had a girlfriend or female lover. We also use some good stories with nothing to indicate the man is bi as opposed to gay. If a story seems more suited for one of our gay magazines, we'll use it there. (Pay rates are the same.)

We require that hot stories about men either are set pre-1980 or include the practice of only "safe sex" (most frequently, wearing a condom; other safe sex acts also welcome). Please note that we do not deem unprotected oral to be "safe" even if the man withdraws prior to ejaculating.

Rate of pay for articles and stories is $100 for all rights, payable on publication. We pay promptly and will reassign book rights on request after the story has been published. We will not consider simultaneous submissions. We are not buying "letters" at this time.

We are distributed in Canada. Canadian censorship restrictions make the following things taboo: underage (must be 18 or over), incest (including sex between relatives not related by blood, e.g. in-laws or step-relatives), golden showers and scat, degradation or humiliation, B&D, S&M, rape, bestiality, and a few other things you're not likely to write about. We also do not wish to see references to drug use or to members of the clergy.

Please pick one name for a body part and stick to it throughout that story (i.e. "dick" or "prick" or "cock," "pussy" or "cunt").

Manuscripts submitted to Options will automatically be considered for our gay magazines, including Beau and other titles, if suitable. Pay rate is the same at all.

You can reach us online at DianaEditr@AOL.com. (Address is for editorial dept. only.) It's perfectly OK to submit manuscripts electronically as attached textfiles.

YOUNG AND TIGHT GUIDELINES

Stories for Young & Tight should be 2000 words and get to the heat within 500 words, sustaining the heat for the rest of the story except for perhaps one paragraph or so of wrap-up at the end. Stories should be about a girl of around18 or 19, possibly but not necessarily a college student, possibly but not necessarily a virgin up till the encounter described in the story. She can be involved in an encounter with a boy her own age or an "older" (perhaps mid-thirties) guy. Story may be told either from the girl's viewpoint or the guy's.

"Ambisexters' Club" features run to 1000 words, with perhaps one paragraph or so of lead-in before you get to the heat. Each issue features a different girl's story about an encounter with another girl. These girls are bi, not lesbian.

All stories/features are written in the first person, as if true. If written from the girl's point of view, it's good if you can have her write in the teen vernacular. If written from the guy's point of view, it's good if the girl, when speaking, utilizes some teentalk, if only a word or two here or there.

Please pick one name per body part (pussy/cunt/cunny, dick/prick/cock) per story and stick to it throughout.

Note that in order to have our female characters maintain a semblance of youthfulness, we don't want them to have big boobs. Please do not, however, portray them in such a way that they appear underage. I realize we're asking you to walk a fine line, but that's the way it has to be.

The magazine is distributed in Canada, so please observe the Canadian censorship taboos, which include B&D, S&M, menstrual sex, sex with a pregnant woman, golden showers, incest, spanking, dominance, humiliation, degradation, rape, bestiality, and underage. In addition to the Canadian taboos, we also do not want references to clergy or to any drugs.

Pay is $100 for stories, $50 for "Ambisexters" features, payable on publication. We do not consider simultaneous submissions; we respond very promptly, normally within three weeks, so there is no reason to submit elsewhere at the same time. Submissions may be made in the form of hardcopy, preferably with a disk enclosed, or as an attached textfile via e-mail. SASE must be enclosed for notification (and return of disk) even if manuscript is disposable. If submitting or corresponding by e-mail, the address is: DianaEditr@aol.com.

YOUNG AND TIGHT FANTASIES GUIDELINES

Young and Tight Fantasies uses primarily "letters," with, at present, only one story in each issue. Letters should be as close to 1000 words each as possible. Stories should be 2000 words.

Letters need to get right into the hot action with a minimum of set-up or intro; no more than two or three sentences of set up, please, with the balance of the letter hot. Stories need to get to the heat within 500 words, sustaining the heat for the rest of the story except for perhaps one paragraph or so of wrap-up at the end, only if needed.

The main female character in all manuscripts should be a girl of 18 or 19. The guy can be her age or older; in a lesbian or bi story, the other woman can also be 18 or 19 or can be older. In a threesome story the other girl should ideally be 18 or 19 too. These girls can be but do not have to be college students. Story/letter may be told either from the girl's viewpoint or the guy's. We want a mix of both.

All stories/letters are written in the first person, as if true. If it's written from the girl's point of view, and you are conversant with current teen vernacular, you can use it lightly; don't be heavy-handed. If you're not comfortable with teen expressions, don't attempt them. Don't attempt to convey youth through such device as throwing a lot of "like's and such into the letter. Most don't *write* that way, and even if they did, in a real letter we'd edit it out. If you are quoting *spoken dialogue,* it's okay to have someone *speak* that way.

Please pick one name per body part (pussy/cunt/cunny, dick/prick/cock) per story and stick to it throughout.

Note that in order to have our female characters seem youthful, we don't want most to have big boobs. We will print a very few letters about girls with big boobs, to satisfy readers whose tastes run along those lines.

Please do not, however, portray the girls in such a way that they appear underage.

And please do refer to them as "girls" (or "chicks," "honeys," "babes," or "gals") rather than "women" or "young women."

The magazine is distributed in Canada, so please observe the Canadian censorship taboos, which include B&D, S&M, menstrual sex, sex with a pregnant woman, golden showers, incest, spanking, dominance, humiliation, degradation, rape, bestiality, and underage. In addition to the Canadian taboos, we also do not want references to clergy or to *any* drugs.

Pay is $100 for stories, $20 for letters, payable on publication. We do not consider simultaneous submissions; we respond very promptly, normally within three weeks, so there is no reason to submit elsewhere at the same time. Submissions may be made in the form of hardcopy with a disk enclosed, or as an attached textfile via e-mail. SASE must be enclosed for notification (and return of disk) even if manuscript is disposable. Nothing will be accepted that is not available on disk or as attached textfile.

If submitting or corresponding by e-mail, the address is: DianaEditr@aol.com

If sending by mail, please address to:

Diana Sheridan, Editor,
Young & Tight Fantasies
Bridge Street Publishing Group
P.O. Box 170
Irvington NY 10533

Categorized Book & Magazine Listings

Oh, how I wish this list had been around when I first started writing porn! Lucky as I was to live near a large newsstand with an extensive selection of porn, it was still quite a chore to sift through all the magazines on the shelf, looking for new markets. The markets below are (as of this writing) magazines and books that feature editorial content. From fiction to letters to non-fiction, they're all potential outlets for your work.

I've included as much of the most recent contact and content information for each one as possible. Start by requesting guidelines and sample copies of those titles that you're most interested in. While nothing can take the place of seeing and reading each magazine, this list can be a starting place for you begin to compile your own list of working markets..

Amateur

Naughty Neighbors
The Score Group
1629 NW 84 Ave
Miami FL 33126

Asian

Asia 18
210 Route 4 East – Ste 211
Paramus NJ 07625-5116

Asian Beauties
PO Box 335

New York 10118

Going Bust Asian
350 5th Ave
New York NY 10118

Ass

Backdoor
PO Box 170
Irvington NY 10533

Cheeks
210 Route 4 East – Ste 211
Paramus NJ 07625-5116

Tail Ends
Mavety Media Group
462 Broadway Ste 4000
New York NY 10013-2697

Big Bust

Gent
Firestone Publishing
1411 Commerce Wy Ste 420
Miami Lakes FL 33016-1598

Hustler Busty Beauties
L.F.P. Inc.
8484 Wilshire Blvd Ste 900
Beverly Hills CA 90211

Juggs

Mavety Media Group
462 Broadway Ste 4000
New York NY 10013-2697

Score
The Score Group
1629 NW 84 Ave
Miami FL 33126

Big

Voluptuous
The Score Group
1629 NW 84 Ave
Miami FL 33126

Black

Black Pleasures
PO Box 90
RCS NY 10019

Black Tail
Tux Magazine, Inc
462 Broadway – 4th floor
New York NY 10013

Chocolate Creem
(See complete listing under **Paying Markets**)

Hot Chocolate
Global Productions, Inc
401 Broadway
New York NY 10013

Players Black Legs
8060 Melrose Ave
Los Angeles CA 90046

Players Nasty
8060 Melrose Ave
Los Angeles CA 90046

Celebrity

Celebrity Skin
PO Box 10531
Rockville MD 10531

Celebrity Sleuth
801 2nd Ave
New York NY 10017

Couple

Penthouse Variations
General Media International
277 Park Ave 4th floor
New York NY 10172-0099

Fetish

Assertive Women
153 W 27th – Rm 1005
New York NY 10001

Bondage Fantasies
(See complete listing under **Paying Markets**)

Boudoir Noir
(See complete listing under **Paying Markets**)

Comic Fantasies
(See complete listing under **Paying Markets**)

Extreme Fetish
1360 Clifton Ave – Ste 327
Clinton NJ 07012

Fetish Bazaar
(See complete listing under **Paying Markets**)

Fetish Magazine
Hawke Int'l Pub
170 Clara St
San Francisco CA 94107-1121

Hustler's Taboo
LFP Inc
8484 Wilshire Blvd Ste 900
Beverly Hills CA 90211

Nugget
Firestone Publishing
14411 Commerce Wy Ste 420
Miami Lakes Fl 33016-1598

For Women

Playgirl
801 2nd Ave 19th floor
New York NY 10017-4706

Whap!
Retro Systems
PO Box 69461
Los Angeles CA 90069

Gay

Beau
(See complete listing under **Paying Markets**)

Boy Next Door
(See complete listing under **Paying Markets**)

Cherry Boys
(See complete listing under **Paying Markets**)

Coming Out
(See complete listing under **Paying Markets**)

First Hand
PO Box 1314
Teaneck NJ 07666

Grizzly
PO Box 170
Irvington NY 10533

Indulge for Men
13122 Saticoy St
Hollywood CA 91605

General

American Sex Scene
(See complete listing under **Paying Markets**)

Batteries Not Included
(See complete listing under **Non Paying Markets**)

Blowfish Update
(See complete listing under **Paying Markets**)

Cheri
801 2nd Ave
New York NY 10017

Chic
LFP Inc
8484 Wilshire Blvd Ste 900
Beverly Hills CA 90211

Clean Sheets
(See complete listing under **Paying Markets**)

Club
Paragon Publishing
Box 380
Sandy Hook CT 06482-0380

Eidos
(See complete listing under **Non Paying Markets**)

Erotica Magazine
1303 Underwood Ave
San Francisco CA 94124

Erotasy

(See complete listing under **Paying Markets**)

Fox
Montcalm Publishing Corp
401 Park Ave. South
New York NY 10016-8802

Gallery
Montcalm Publishing Corp
401 Park Ave. South
New York NY 10016-8802

Genesis
(See complete listing under **Paying Markets**)

High Society
801 2nd Ave Rm 705
New York NY 10017-4706

Hot Talk (Penthouse)
General Media International
277 Park Ave 4th floor
New York NY 10172-0099

Hustler
L.F.P., Inc.
8484 Wilshire Blvd Ste 900
Beverly Hills CA 90211

Hustler Fantasies
L.F.P., Inc.
8484 Wilshire Blvd Ste 900
Beverly Hills CA 90211

Hustler Humor
L.F.P., Inc.
8484 Wilshire Blvd Ste 900
Beverly Hills CA 90211

Hustler's Hometown Girls
L.F.P., Inc.
8484 Wilshire Blvd Ste 900
Beverly Hills CA 90211

Naughty Neighbors
The Score Group
1629 NW 84 Ave
Miami FL 33126

Not Quite A Webzine
(See complete listing under **Non Paying Markets**)

Oceania Limited
(See complete listing under **Paying Markets**)

Oui
Princeton Publishing
12 W 27th St 14th Floor
New York NY 10001

Playboy
680 N Lake Shore Dr
Chicago IL 60611

Penthouse
General Media International
277 Park Ave 4th floor
New York NY 10172-0099

Qlimax Times
(See complete listing under **Paying Markets**)

Swank
Swank Publications
210 Route 4 E Ste 401
Paramus NJ 07652

Tight
Mavety Media Group
462 Broadway Ste 4000
New York NY 10013-2697

Velvet
Magna Publishing
210 Rte 4 East - Ste 401
Paramus NJ 07652-5103

GLBT

Lambda Book Report
(See complete listing under **Paying Markets**)

Options
(See complete listing under **Paying Markets**)

Hispanic

Hot Latinas
(See complete listing under **Paying Markets**)

Legs and Feet

Hustler's Leg World
L.F.P., Inc.
8484 Wilshire Blvd Ste 900
Beverly Hills CA 90211

Leg Sex
(See complete listing under **Paying Markets**)

Leg Show
462 Broadway – 4th Floor
New York NY 10013

Leg Tease
153 W 27th St – Rm 1005
New York NY 10001

Players Black Legs
8060 Melrose Ave
Los Angeles CA 90046

Natural

Perfect 10

Voluptuous
The Score Group
4931 SW 75 Ave
Miami FL 33155

Older Women

30Something
The Score Group
1629 NW 84 Ave
Miami FL 33126

She-Male

She-Male Magic
One Metro Park Dr
Cranston RI 02910

Small

Petite
Firestone Publishing Inc
14411 Commerce Wy Ste 420
Hialeah FL 33016

Small Tops

Transgender

Transformation
Vista Station
PO Box 51480
Sparks NV 89435-1480
Attn: Jeri

Younger Women

Babe
Mavety Media Group
462 Broadway Ste 4000
New York NY 10013-2697

BabyFace
The Score Group
1629 NW 84 Ave
Miami FL 33126

Barely 18
#4 Chelsea Point
Dana Point CA 92629

Candy Girls
Dowager Inc
801 2nd Ave
New York NY 10017

Finally Legal
801 2nd Ave
New York NY 10017

Hawk
801 2nd Ave
New York NY 10017

Hustler's Barely Legal
L.F.P., Inc.
8484 Wilshire Blvd Ste 900
Beverly Hills CA 90211

Just 18
(See complete listing under **Paying Markets**)

Just Come of Age
PO Box 685
Amityville NY 11701

Lollypops
Montcalm Publishing Corp
401 Park Ave. South
New York NY 10016-8802

Panty Girls
REV International, Inc.
PO Box 685
Amityville NY 11701

Panty Play
Mavety Media Group
462 Broadway Ste 4000
New York NY 10013-2697

Purely 18
801 2nd Ave
New York NY 10017

Teenz
8060 Melrose Ave
Los Angeles CA 90046

Young and Tight
(See complete listing under **Paying Markets**)

Young and Tight Fantasies
(See complete listing under **Paying Markets**)

Books

Best Women's Erotica
(See complete listing under **Paying Markets**)

Herotica
(See complete listing under **Paying Markets**)

Internet

Erotasy
(See complete listing under **Paying Markets**)

Not Quite A Webzine
(See complete listing under **Non Paying Markets**)

Acknowledgements

First and foremost I'd like to thank my husband for his absolute and unconditional support of my writing career. He's done it all - from taking on extra jobs to support us to insisting that I not sell out by getting a *real* job to performing the rather tedious job of proofreading each and every manuscript. Without his support none of this would have been possible. Ok, so maybe it would have been possible but it wouldn't have been nearly as much fun.

Thanks to my children, who aren't even sure exactly what it is that I write but still proudly say *Mommy's a writer* when asked what their mother does at home all day.

Thanks to John and The Score Group for your unfailing professionalism and thanks especially to Gabi and Bruce for your assignments and kind words and of course for those incredibly melodious accents. Thanks Angela for getting me started on this particular path, who'd a thunk it?

Thanks to the friends and computer geeks and family who've been so supportive, Greg (Westward Ho, indeed), Jeremy (who never calls but I love him anyway) Liz (for such beautiful artwork), Laurie (she of many characters, including that of "Mz. Santa Claus" to my children) Rob (computer geek above *all* others) and all the school moms who think that what I do is cool, not perverted.

ABOUT KATY TERREGA

Katy Terrega has been writing and publishing porn for over ten years. She has contributed fiction, letters and articles to publications such as Gallery, Penthouse Variations, Score, and Hustler, to name just a few. She also maintains a website – http://www.KatyTerrega.com - that features her short stories and is the editor of a newsletter for aspiring as well as professional porn/erotica writers.

She resides in Colorado with her husband and two children